GENTLEMEN DON'T RUN

ALISTER AUSTIN

To Richard Austin and his wonderful humour

1

Friday, June 15th 1923

Everything is black.

I am naked and alone. Only my abject terror for company.

Out of the dark, it strikes again. Reduces me to rubble.

'Mercy. Mercy,' I cry pathetically – but there's barely a moment's rest before the noise, the bone-splintering reverberations are back, washing over me in violent, nausea-inducing waves. Terrified and with my cowardice exhausted, I decide to stop hiding. Nobly, I open my eyes – the effort very nearly overwhelming.

I find I am horizontal and looking right down the barrel of my body. My head, propped up on pillows, sits at a violent right angle to the rest of me. I'm dressed, I note. Well dressed, naturally. There is vomit on me, though. Vomit on my chest – yesterday's crusts and some mint leaves, I should imag-

Owwww – I manage to emote before emoting no more, beset as I am by another violent battery. The noise, coupled with the sharp virgin light, is all too much. My world wobbles, then shatters, before slowly and painfully coalescing.

I concentrate outside of me. The wall beyond my Oxfords sharpens into focus. The armoire opposite, doors asunder and littered with heavily dented bottles, anchors me in the now... I sense a presence to my left. Marshalling my courage, I turn my head. It doesn't budge an inch. The muscles, it would seem, have long since seized up. Can't say I blame them.

Determinedly, I grind my eyes to the left, crunching grit as they go. I scrape my vision across the armoire, the alcohol, the pills, powders, tinctures and tonics – until finally it comes to rest upon a man.

He's sat bolt upright in a chair. Dead, to the untrained eye. He too is well dressed. He too, a mess. An empty bottle of scotch – its leaked contents having further scumbled his already soiled shirt – peeks out from its resting place inside a sweat-crusted armpit; a needle, embedded to the hilt, dangles from a forearm; a cigarette is afixed to the dried spittle about his mouth; and his glassy, bloodshot eyes are set wide and paranoid.

I regard him for a goodly moment and he never blinks. Maybe he really has given up the ghost. No. I've seen the dead, and even the worst of 'em are decent enough to have some peace about them – and if not peace, at least quiet. There's nothing quiet about this brute. All anguish and twisted vice.

'THE NOISE!' I croak at him.

'You be s*th*ilent, you beastly wretch!' it snarls, spittle frothing about the mouth, the lips never moving.

'THE NOISE!' I retort.

'You are the noise!'

I stop. An unnerving thought.

'I'm the noise?'

'Ye*sssstthhhh*.'

'I'm the noiiiissse?'

'It's in your bloody head.'

'It's in my head? It's in my head!' I gasp. 'It's. In. My. Head.'

'Ye*ssssttthhh*.'

I try this out for size once more. I'm nearly there... 'It's in my head. It's my head... IT'S MY HEAD!'

'Ye*ssssttthhhh*,' it wheezes once more, exasperated and pleased in equal parts by my retarded realisation.

'I'LL GIVE YOU SOMETHING TO WHINE ABOUT, YOU BASTARD!' I cry.

Gathering the few granules of energy I have left, I fling a limp arm to the right. I feel it land on the bedside drawers, accompanied by the sound of breaking glass. Spider-like, my hand explores the top until it grasps an object. I heave it back to me and raise the bottle to my line of vision. My bloodied hand has smeared the label – I can't make it out. Not that it matters. The drums thunder once more. A great anger surges inside me: there is no greater betrayal than to be turned upon by one's own body.

Shakily, I raise the bottle to my lips. There's a good two fifths inside. *Enough to do the job*, I think happily. The bottle flips vertically and begins to drain. Gin. Thank you, Lord.

I suckle away contentedly. The last few gulps prove too much – they overflow and spill down my face. It's warm, inviting.

As the drumming recedes, along with consciousness, I mumble 'That'll show… I… me, milk.' And off I drift.

* * *

Breakfast is a poor affair. I gaze out the window. To look elsewhere is to risk eye contact with the patrons of this so-called country club – a bunch of glorified costermongers and nothing more. It's clear why artists paint the countryside in Cornwall and not the people.

Carefully, I cut the crust off my toast. Then, spearing a single side of the crust, I brush it – nay, merely waft it – across the unbroken yolk of my egg. Salt, pepper and down it goes. Its passage is smooth. I decide on another side of crust.

Terrence appears. The man from my room. Our room. He looks a lot less corpse-like now, although an air of death does linger on in his complexion. He looks at my plate, the unbroken egg, the two sides of missing crust. 'Oh, you've already eaten, Egbert. I s*th*ay, couldn't you wait?'

'I did try to wake you. You were dead to the world,' I reply.

'Your usual dish, sir?' our server enquires. Terrence nods. The server is already prepared: from a tray he presents Terrence with a single piece of ice, garnished with thyme.

'Ex*th*ellent,' says Terrence, popping it in his mouth and sucking. 'Now that we've broken fas*tht*, how about a drink at the beach? Bleed out the bile.'

'I say,' I say to the waiter. 'I say, you wouldn't happen to have a bandage, would you?' My hand is still bleeding, the linen tablecloth practically dyed claret.

* * *

My toes sift sand as I recline. My blue view is interrupted by the occasional scudding cloud. I've given up on my paper – the words won't stick. It's warm out, but the breeze takes the edge off. The seagulls' cries are a damn nuisance though. I drink.

'The sun. The beach. The fresh sea air. Makes*th* a man whole again.'

'Mmmmmmm,' I reply to Terrence.

'Sir?'

Terrence slurps noisily on a gin and tonic. Terrence is a large man, both in height and width – like a great big ball of smooth lard, with a fat moustache and an even fattier liver.

He talks with the most peculiar impediment: the Rs and Ss of his speech being interchangeably, but never consistently, interfered with. One would almost believe he adopted it for effect. In fact, he was the only person I knew whose speech *improved* in direct proportion to that of their insobriety. I would have been convinced it was a lie, one he wouldn't even confide to me, if I hadn't witnessed first hand on numerous occasions his lisping and laboured mispronunciations while muttering in his sleep; when completely inebriated; and in any other situation where he was found to be consciously dormant to the world. Impediments to one side, he has a tonal quality that sounds like a frog dangling from a noose.

'*Weeeeelax*ation,' groans Terrence.

'Sir?' our boy helper says once more. He's not much of a help, but he's the best we can get in the circumstances.

'Now, Timmy, don't interrupt,' Terrence warns. 'We're *wee*-laxing.'

'But, sir!'

'Thin ic*the*, boy.'

Timmy's eyes flick nervously between us and something behind. 'Begging your pardon, sirs, but we gotta move, them fellas behind have caught up!'

Unfazed, we look behind us to see a rowdy group of golfers striding towards our sand bunker, waving their sticks in agitation. Not our fault if they can't keep their balls on the straight and narrow.

'Awfully close, Timmy. Do speak up sooner nex*tht* time.'

We stride to the next sand bunker, little Timmy in tow with deckchairs, tray, drinks, tonics, and cases. I carry the newspaper – he doesn't even thank me.

'I say, Terrence…'

'Ye*sth*, Eggy?'

'It'd be much simpler if we just went to the actual beach – it's only down the way.'

'*Th*ertainly not. Full of commoners. Lord knows what we'd catch down there.'

'Nothing that you don't already have, I'm sure.'

'Oh, I'm not speaking of the lustful kind, rather dis*theasthes* of the mind. Dangerous to s*thocth*iety to be mixing with those sorts,' warns Terrence.

'Never stopped you before, you old goat.'

'Not when one's recuperating, Eggy, defences lowered. Do you know how the G*w*eat War started?'

'Yes, it was over my childhood sweetheart.'

'The Archduke F*w*anz Ferdinand,' Terrence continues, 'was taking his ease in his car, guard *w*ee-laxed, when Gav-*w*ee-lo P*w*ins*th*ip, A COMMON MAN, walked up and s*th*hot him. Now, I don't know this Fwanz chap – maybe he did deserve the heave-ho, I don't know, don't know the man – but I DO know that you can't have a commoner doing it; dis*th*rupts the natural balance of things.'

'Are you afraid of being shot?'

'Don't you think I'd rather be down there, Eggy? On the beach, chasing some skirt. I'd move through it like a train on a slope. But sometimes we have to look at the bigger picture, do what's right by s*th*oc*th*iety.'

'Well said, Tear. Very decent.'

'Thank you, I do try.'

We mount a small grassy mound. Terrence pauses at its summit, legs firmly planted and hands on hips – like a conquering hero. He's squeezed into a striped bathing suit, taut and lumpy as it strains against his considerable girth. Sandals and socks finish the look. With narrowed eyes he takes in the view: the course, the beach, the sea, the people. Nodding to himself, 'I'd plough through them like a scythe through wheat.'

2

Saturday, June 16th 1923

We're back at the sand bunkers. It's a new day. But it's really just the same day. The words of my paper still won't stick, so I've decided on tea. A pot rests on a table between us.

'Time for a little pick-me-up, me thinks*th*.' Terrence reaches towards the tea. 'Have to be quicker with that tea next time, boy. Awfully tepid,' he says to our boy helper while opening a small silver case next to the tea and having a quick snort.

In the boy's defence, he tried his best, but his legs are simply too short to cover the distance in time. His arms are laced with burns from spilling it in the sprint. He bears it well though, as he should. It's character-building. He's jolly grateful for it, I'm sure.

'I quite like my tea tepid. You know where you stand with it.' That's not true, not true at all. Not sure why I said it. God, I must be bored.

I'm not supposed to be here in Cornwall with Terrence. I'm supposed to be in Canada, banking. I know diddly squat about banking. I offer people tea while I reach for their money. That's how I bank. My sister's wedding, however, persuaded me to take a break from tea-drinking in Montreal and return to England.

Seven days of travel landed me in Southampton, with the final leg of my journey depositing me in Bristol just in time for the big day. After which, I travelled with family down to the restorative airs of Bath. Once sufficiently bathed, I planned to shake myself dry and spring upon London, choke down an enriching shot of proper culture – real refinement – before returning west. Touch base in the capital with those who matter: elderly gentlemen with stiff hats and imposing moustaches (you know the type, with pipe smoke so thick it crackles and thunders). Show the dry old codgers how unremarkably splendid I am. Unfortunately, every time I rose from my bathing determined to journey on, a dilatory, dilly-dallying torpidity set upon me and sent me straight back down.

In spite of indulging in all of the restorative elixirs Bath had to offer me, I was unable to shake myself of my malady. Lacking the willpower to do much of anything else, I found myself, day after day, whiling away the sunlit hours pruning in the waters of Bath, the evenings pickling in its bars, waiting for my mood to lift.

And as chance would have it, it was as I brined my innards one night in the hot and humid backroom of the Butcher's Arms that Terrence, like a freshly smoked ham, came crashing through the sweat and the haze. It had been over three years since we had last seen one another, and it had taken some effort to convince Tear that I wasn't merely a humdrum fever-dream of his opium-addled mind.

Over a drink or many, I learnt that Terrence was broke. Not an unusual state of affairs: Terrence is from proper wealth, and when one walks in that rarefied air you'll find that one bleeds money. The game is to catch him and cut him. Tear Bear loves the chase, safe in the knowledge that when he's tired of oozing his father will make all well. Only now his father has tired of the antics and has cut him off entirely, refusing to assist Terrence until he at least makes a decent man of himself and settles down with a wife. Terrence didn't take well to this act of blackmail and instead took to the road, avoiding his creditors while waiting for his old man – who is very much an old man – to die.

All had been going well for Terrence until he imposed himself for too long on the hospitality of the Earl of Buckwald – and, more to the point, Buckwald's sister. In doing so, he crossed a line laid down by his own kind and found himself an outcast abroad in the countryside, with no friends, no money, and a father who is very much alive.

My encounter with Terrence marked the two-month point of his banditry, romping his way around the south-west of England on a diet of fraudulent cheques.

As he continued to serenade me with his trials and tribulations and the sun dropped off from the Somerset sky, the rejuvenating desire to jump in and join Terrence on what seemed to be a jolly old romp began to take hold. A few more drinks were all it took to flush the last of the poison from my soul and free me of my melancholy. Early that next morning – before sober Eggy could intervene, and robed as I was in a new, impetuous optimism – I left my monies and purse behind, and Tear and I set off about the countryside at a frantic pace, trusting Terrence's bad credit and worthless cheques to see us right. My intention was to spend a few days soaking up Tear's lust for life – a week at the very most – and use it as fuel to rocket me to London. Before I knew it, though, a whole fortnight had passed. Hard and heavy we had gone, ever westward, bouncing merrily from hotel to country club until eventually we bounced ourselves into a corner at the very edge of England.

Now, as I stare drunkenly from my deckchair at the changing sky, I'm beginning to wonder if it isn't time to wrap things up. It's been fun Peter Panning around the English countryside, never settling anywhere long enough for word to catch up that Terrence Chalambert is a bent two-bob bit, but we've run out of land to run on and have spent the last few days in a stationary fugue at the tippy tip of Cornwall. All good things must come to an end, I suppose, and in this desolate backwater of the realm I imagine all good things do indeed die a death.

Perhaps it's time to return to Montreal, to the bank. Six weeks' leave I took, and it's already been four – in hindsight, I can't help but think that I've wasted much of it. If I push off now, I should make it back with a few days to spare; might stand me in good stead with those at the top, show I'm committed.

I'm not like Tear. I do need to work. Or at least, I need to appear to work – which is precisely what I do. Fortunately, I've learnt that most bankers are as clueless as I am on how it all operates: money, banking. I find that as long as one dresses respectably, knows one's classics, and exhibits opinions that are equally condescending of the poor and judgemental of the rich, one will do quite nicely… which is a fine thesis to live by when you're there, but the more time I spend away the more I become acutely aware that someone may register that my absence has resulted in no extra work for anyone whatsoever. Lordy, productivity may have actually increased, along with a definite uptick in client satisfaction. Worse still, they may discover that with me gone they're no longer haemorrhaging money on tea and lunch. (I do take long lunches.)

Curse it! I've set myself off worrying. I've developed a gentle perspiration… that's it then. No point stewing. Time to stop delaying the inevitable and get a move on. A man as water-starved as me shouldn't be thinking himself into a sweat – there lies a dry death.

It'll be a shame not to see London, but honestly it really wouldn't be worth it to go for just a *few* days. London can be perilously intoxicating. A single day spent in London and a whole week may pass elsewhere. One goes for a long weekend and leaves old and grey. I have the *bank* to think about.

A cloud in the shape of a horse goes scudding by as I pluck up the courage to inform Tear that our jolly romp has hit a Cornish rut. I always hate leaving. Or rather I hate goodbyes – they make me feel guilty. Maybe I'll wait until he's well on, completely occupied by the bottle, then head off to relieve myself and simply not return. That's how I prefer to do it, whenever possible… I'll leave him a note, of course: '*Gone back to Canada. Eggy.*'

Only problem with this plan is that if I wait for Terrence to get nice and tight, I'll be nice and tight myself… Oh, sod it. Let's just wrap up this whole shameful bingeing adventure right now, call it a day

'Off for a tinkle, old bean,' I say to Terrence, standing.

'*W*ight you are,' replies Tear with a glance, before returning to a state of extreme leisure.

I make to shuffle off but I've barely taken a step when I feel Terrence's focus lock back onto me, his gaze piercing me from behind like hot pokers.

Lordy, does he suspect? I dismiss the thought as quickly as it appears. *Don't be silly, Eggy. He knows nothing. Just keep moving, casual as you like. You'll be fine…* Except I'm not casual, am I? I'm stewing. Even more so now. I've taken not even three steps, but I've managed to get myself thoroughly worked up. Oh, Lord. This is why I normally abscond under cover of darkness. I'm an exceptionally guilty person.

I steal a look back at Tear just to make sure he hasn't noticed – I can't help myself!

Dash it. He has noticed. Our eyes meet. Terrence registers the tremor in my legs, the sweat accumulating profusely on my brow.

'…Goodbye…' I hear myself squawk involuntarily, really panicked now. I turn quickly back around, preparing to run.

'Eggy?' calls Tear, sounding thoroughly confused, maybe even a little concerned. My legs turn instantly to lead. *Damn it. He's got me.*

Twisting at the hips, feet rooted to the spot, drawn against my will, I rotate to face Tear once more. Desperately, I try to resist. One last push to stay strong, not to collapse, to stand tall… but naturally, I crumble.

'I… I think it's time to leave,' I weep, ashamedly.

'The golf cours*th*e?'

'No… the country.'

'S*th*ay it isn't so, Eggy. Do you have to?'

'Fraid so. Don't want to. Do have to,' I sob, snottily.

'I thought you had a few weeks*th* yet?'

'Yes, well. Probably best to get back just in case there's… traffic. Wouldn't do to be late.'

'Oh...'

'Yes.'

I feel terrible. This is all my fault. I should have waited until nightfall, left a note.

'What will you do now, old bean?' I ask, juxtaposing my tears with forced cheer.

'Oh, you know. Fight the good fight,' responds Tear with equally forced enthusiasm.

'That's good,' I reply, lamely. I suspect that with me gone Tear will, in actual fact, throw in the towel. Probably return home, beg daddy for absolution and be married before summer's out. Perhaps if he hadn't met me he would have persevered with his escapades, but seeing me head off back to the real world, leaving him to wallow in Cornish squalor, has to be a bitter tonic to swallow.

Tear's trying to formulate an argument for me to stay when the fragile sound of 'Mr Chalambert! Mr Chalambert!' interrupts us.

'Sir, there's a man approaching,' our burnt boy snivels.

'Does he have any clubs*th*?' asks Tear, still preoccupied with trying to keep me here.

'No.'

'Good. Because I'm not moving.'

'Mr Chalambert! Mr Chalambert!' the voice calls again. This time it's close enough to be recognisable, and Terrence pales at the realisation. He takes a moment and then bolts – a surprisingly explosive leap, his flesh rippling under the forces. It takes me a fraction longer but recognition dawns on me too. Quickly, I stick out a foot and trip the fleeing fat man. After my failure at a cowardly escape, I'm determined for Terrence not to outshine me.

'No, Tear. Steady now,' I say as he tumbles to the ground. 'It's just Jenkins, Tear Bear,' I reassure him.

'If he can find me, so can my creditos,' squeals Tear.

'Oh, I doubt that, sirs,' cuts in Jenkins, pleased with himself. 'Very difficult to locate you. The address you left sent me on quite the goose chase.'

Jenkins has a voice like old dry leaves, giving the impression he might turn to dust at any moment. Lord knows how old he is, but I strongly suspect that he should be dead.

'What's the meaning of this, Jenkins? Sneaking up on me, you old creep. You scared the s*thensthesth* out of me.'

'My apologies, sir.'

'How the devil did you find me? I'm a wanted man.'

'Matter of chance in the end, sir. I was on the train back from Wales, where I'd been searching, when I happened to spot a discarded Cornish newspaper…' It's a long story, and a dull one. I tune him out. After a good fistful of spirit to soothe my sweaty brow, a splash of tepid tea for hydration, and a smidge of the white stuff, I sense Jenkins wrapping up. '… the artist's rendering wasn't entirely accurate, but I'd recognise that nose anywhere, sir,' finishes Jenkins.

Terrence's eyes narrow. 'Once I found out why you've disturbed me, I'm going to beat you like a dog, Jenkins.'

'It's your father, sir,' responds Jenkins – unfazed, the senile old goat.

'What does that cruel bas*th*tard want?'

'Nothing, sir. He's dead, sir.'

'Good God,' Terrence gasps. 'Did you hear that, Eggy? Dead.'

Good God indeed, I heard it well enough. Dead. Will you look at that? Just as I thought Terrence's adventure was sure to die a dull death, his father dies instead. At the thirteenth hour, circumstance has come barrelling to Tear's rescue with life's ace of spades: an old, dead, rich man. What a fantastic turn of events. I feel it unbecoming to show my pleasure in a time of mourning though, and so I reply with a solemn, 'Indeed I heard, Terrence. God rest his soul.' I dip my fingers in my gin and splash the sign of the cross. That should do it.

'I'm wealthy again.' Greedy pleasure is smeared across Tear's fleshy cheeks.

'Blessings be upon you, Tear Bear.' I splash some more gin.

'When's the funeral, Jenkins?'

'Yesterday, sir. The will requested you not be present, for fear of a scene.'

'A sound request,' I note.

'Yeeeesssss*ttttthhhhh*. The will. By Jove, how wealthy shall I be?' salivates Terrence.

'Well, that's the thing, sir. That's why I'm here. The will, it has – how did he put it? – conditions, sir. It has certain requirements that must be met or you forfeit your right to it,' explains Jenkins.

'THAT BAS*TH*TARD!' explodes Tear Bear.

'God rest his soul.' I splash another gin cross. Never pays to ignore the proprieties.

'The condition is nothing much if you ask me, sir. Your father simply stated that you be present for the signing over of the estate.'

'That's it?'

'Why, yes sir.'

'What happens to the money if I don't meet the requirements*th*?'

'If you're not present, control of the estate, along with your portion of the monies, is given to your sister, Ms Chalambert.'

'That s*th*our-faced bitch?! I'd *w*ather give it to the poor. When's the signing?'

'Your father ordered it to be held seven days from the date of his death, sir.'

'From his death? How long did it take you to find me?'

'A mere four days, sir.'

'So, three days left. Bet he timed it with my departure, miserable old goat.'

'May he rest in peace.' Gin cross.

'I had no idea you were so pious*th*, Eggy.'

'Indeed,' I acknowledge, graciously.

'Well, what say you?' asks Tear. 'Fancy s*th*neaking back to London with me? One last hurrah. Let me cash in my winnings*th* and I'll give you a proper send-off.'

By Jove, London – with Tear Bear. That's more like it. Now

that I think about it, a *few* days is all one needs in London. No need to overdo it.

I don't want to come across over-eager though, and so I respond with a pensive, pained, 'Ooooh. I really don't know, old bean.'

'I'll have you on the boat back wes*th*t before the Friday coming. You have my word, Eggy.'

I don't respond, artfully drawing out my decision. 'Lis*th*en, Eggy. It wouldn't pay to show up early in…'

'…Montreal.'

'Mont*w*eal. Wouldn't pay at all. Looks des*th*perate. Tells them that you're overly cautious*th*. Frightened, even. If anything, it would be best to a*ww*ive a few days late. Let them know you run to your own clock and it's never a beat wrong.' It's a powerful logic Tear operates under. Nevertheless, I play it cool for just a moment longer. 'Oh alright, I can s*th*ee you can't be persuaded. Never mind.'

'NO! Wait. No. I'll come. I'll come. Yep… let's… have at it.'

'Oh, s*th*plendid.'

'Well, if you don't mind, sirs, I shall be leaving you to it,' interrupts Jenkins, suddenly coming to life. Good grief, I forgot he was still with us. The man's like a lizard: once he goes still, you've lost him.

'Of course we bloody mind,' snaps Tear. 'You'll stay here and ensure we get nic*th*e and tight. Then in the morning you'll book us on to the first train back. We'll s*th*neak into London, hide out for a few days, receive my dues and then I'll give those wolves something to howl about.'

'Wish I could help, Mr Chalambert, but I'm under explicit orders not to assist you. My inheritance depends on it.'

The air turns icy on the back of Terrence's look. 'Your inheritanc*the*,' he whispers. 'YOUR INHERITANC*TTTHHH*E,' he repeats, exploding in rage and disgust, his pig-like eyes mere pinpricks piercing out from his shaking jowls. 'You greedy little toad. Go fetch me a cane, I'm going to beat you like a dog.'

'Now, Tear,' I interject, soothingly, 'it doesn't pay to shoot the messenger. Even if the messenger is Jenkins. Let's have a drink or three. Celebrate your father's sad demise, God rest him,' – gin cross – 'and in the morning, London.'

* * *

We're in our room, packing. Terrence used to have a man for this sort of thing, but we had to trade him for our losses at a cockfighting ring outside of Chittlehampton. There was no room for negotiation with those boys. They were not to be trifled with.

Packing consists of sorting the unopened bottles, jars, flasks and phials from the opened ones. Any opened but unfinished receptacle is emptied out into a large crockpot in the centre of the room. It's quite the brew we've made.

'I say, Tear, isn't this all a bit ridiculous: a deadline, forfeiting your inheritance, control of the estate?' I ask as I safely stow our seventh and final bottle of untampered gin.

'Oh, quite ridiculous*th*. He was a ridiculous*th* man.'

'But would they do it if you were late? Surely no one would adhere to it. It's your birth right.'

'Oh, they'll do it all *w*ight. In the long and s*th*ordid his*th*tory of my family lineage this is really quite minor. My g*w*eat, g*w*eat, g*w*eat Uncle James insisted his body should be baked in a pie and floated out to sea. And my g*w*eat, g*w*eat, lord-knows-how-many-g*w*eats g*w*and pappy, Richard, declared that should he die on a Tuesday we must invade the Channel Islands – and they did! Mind you, you could in those days. No, I'm afraid there's precedent, Eggy. It's the same firm that's handled my family's matters since the plague. They never waver, they never budge. They're paid far too hands*th*omely.'

'I thought he wanted you to have a wife, not be poor?'

'Yes*th*, indeed, but now he's dead there's nothing to stop me going ahead and marrying a whore. No, this is the g*w*eatest insult he could have left me. It's g*w*eat because it's completely t*w*ivial.

He's saying that he has such a low opinion of me that he doesn't even believe I can be on time to my own inheritance. I have to give it to the canny old bas*th*tard. He's got me. After all, what kind of rebuttal can I fire back now that he's dead? He wins.'

Terrence swabs the corners of an empty tin with a fat finger before smearing his gums with the fine residue it's collected. 'It's not the same you know, the quality,' says Tear, frowning at the tin's label. 'Never has been. Not s*th*ince that meddling Canadian Major whipped up a panic. Never did I fear more for the war effort, Eggy, than when Harrods bowed to pressure and pulled it from their care packages. It's one thing to be s*th*ent over the top, entirely another to do it while withdrawing from cocaine.'

Quality aside, it is an impressive medicinal collection Tear's amassed. He has some rare specimens. It's damn hard to get much of anything stronger than a stiff drink these days.

'Puritans,' spouts Tear scornfully. 'How dare they pres*th*ume to tell us what's good for us and what's not. I was raised religiously on Halls' cocaine lollipops, Eggy – to cure my s*th*weet tooth – and they never did me any harm. It didn't work, obviously. But I can't say, in all hones*th*ty, it didn't help make me the man I am today. Think of all the children who have now been *w*obbed of the same head start.'

'Indeed,' I respond, pouring the last of the opened receptacles, a dusty bottle of Armbrecht Coca Wine, into the crockpot. Terrence reaches for the ladle and gives it a quick stir.

'*W*ight,' says Terrence, raising the ladle to his lips, 'let's plough through this witch's potion as quick as we can, grab an early night, and be ready at the station at dawn for the firs*th*t train back.'

* * *

My enlarged heart beats to a jarring rhythm and the ceiling whirls viciously as I dissolve through my mattress. As I descend, I reflect on today's fine turn of events. If I'm being perfectly honest, my initial impetus to gallivant about the countryside with Tear was fuelled by the assumption that it surely couldn't be much longer until he caved in and headed back to the capital – he's a man of metropolitan life. And I'd rather thought that I'd be much more comfortable returning to London if I went with company. The more we jaunted, though, the more I saw Tear's prodigious stubbornness at work, and thus the more I gave up on *hoping* that Terrence would yield, and the more I started proactively *wishing*. Wishing his father dead. A dead Chalambert would mean an Eggy London.

Ah, London. I drift and sink further, pulled down with memories of my beloved city. In the morning, Cornwall; by lunch, that sickly old lady London.

3

Sunday, June 17th 1923

It's noon. It's Cornwall. We overslept somewhat. The train station is closed, anyway. It transpires that in this god-forsaken corner of England the trains don't run on Sundays. You may think it right and proper of the Cornish people not to slave on God's day, but let me tell you, as a man who has had the misfortune to be in the company of these slovenly peoples, it's not religiosity that keeps them from toil on a Sunday but a lazy, feckless attitude.

Abandoning the train station, we headed back to the club and had them loan us their motorcar. Compared to the refinements offered by a train, a Rolls Royce is little more than a beast of burden, but beggars can't be choosers.

'We'll be lucky to make it past Plymouth in this thing,' complains Terrence.

I couldn't agree more: even if the mechanics hold, my back won't. No sense in us both mithering though. 'Come now, Tear. It made it out here, didn't it?'

'Being pulled by two horses*th*, I should imagine,' responds Terrence.

'Listen,' – time to rally the guard – 'it's an exciting time. Your father's dead.'

'God res*th*t him.'

'Quite,' I say, ashamedly signing a rum cross (note to self, always drink gin in a time of mourning). 'As such, you're champing at the bit –'

'It's t*w*ue,'

'– to get back and seize your fortune.'

'Yes*th*.'

'Crush your enemies underfoot.'

'Quite.'

'Show London what Terrence Chalambert is really made of.'

'Money. I'll be made of money.'

'Well, you can't let nerves get the better of you. How 'bout we get on the road? Unwind. Cheese and crackers.'

'Mmmmmmmm.'

'A cheeky gin.'

'Yes*th*.'

'Splash of whisky.'

'Hmmhmmm.'

'A dram of morphine. By the time the haze lifts we'll be choking on London fog.'

My plan of action does the job. Dark clouds abated, Terrence bounces into the car. I attempt a statelier approach but my body, shaking with anticipation, has other ideas: I career headfirst into the footwell.

We got a little fresh in preparation for the train ride. No sense in boarding sober: trains being the flying Talarias they are, by the time your liver's fallen behind, you're already pulling into the station. And no gent who ever wanted to fit in to fashionable society did it sober: diamond-studded banshees would shred you to pieces. No, best to arrive in a merry state, breathing the fumes of a bottle; that way, if the beast does swallow you whole it's as likely to cough you back up as keep you down.

With no trains in sight, though, and the Rolls still being

prepared, we decided to break for a rum lunch, but the prospect of London had made us giddy – we imbibed a little more than intended, and soon after started to feel sleepy. So, we wolfed down a marching pill apiece – the drawback to that being that the only place one wants to march to is another bit of blow. Fortunately, you can combat that with a few draughts of vintage Sydenham's laudanum – a less experienced hand would assume it's the purity, or perhaps the quantity, of the opium in it that dulls one's cocaine cravings, but it's actually the quality of the sherry used in Sydenham's, their steadfast commitment to the very finest vintage, that makes it such an effective reframer. Reframing the conversation from 'should we do more cocaine?' to '*when* should we do it?' Of course, by the time you've settled on an answer the day has slipped you by and you're in the clear.

And so, by the time we're here in the Rolls, we're a pair of pills each, a good pint of the rum, and a bottle of Sydenham's down.

With difficulty, I clamber up from the floor of the passenger seat footwell and check I still have the note.

Tuesday 19th, 9.00 o'clock, office of Mr Mendelsohn, 16 Lincoln's Inn Fields.

We keep the date and address on each of us, just in case. My note is pinned to the inside of my hat. I dust myself off and shake into my seat. I take a snort more of the good stuff – so much for reframing – and wash it down with Syd. Terrence follows suit. Cocaine is great for clarity, and good lord am I clarified, but its second charm is the ability to speed up the passage of time – and, in doing so, shorten our trip. We may be greedy but we're not stupid.

'*Weady?*' asks Tear. His eyes stare at me beadily from behind the lenses of his driving goggles, while his forehead-fat rolls over the top of the leather, sucking them inwards. He's not driving, of course. He's in the back with me.

'Ready,' I respond, letting out a contented sigh. The thought of being on the road once more; London's siren call, that hacking ethereal cough as it chokes on its own smog, has got me hard. I get comfortable in my seat. I lean my head back and gnaw on my newly sprouted buds of optimism.

Here we go. London, before we know it.

* * *

'JESUS CHRIST,' I scream, or at least I think I do. My cry can't be heard over the bestial roar of the Rolls' tortured engine. And even if I could drum up the required decibels it wouldn't matter – by the time the sound reaches my ears, we've already left.

Lordy, what's happening? I'm not panicked, I'm not spooked, *I'm well beyond that*. I'm filled to the gills with an overwhelming sense of impending doom. *I don't want to die*. I DON'T WANT TO GO.

'Pleeeaaaasssseeeee,' I plead once more. I'm crying. Tears form at the corners of my eyes before being eviscerated by the onslaught of wind. 'I beg you…'

He doesn't respond, doesn't even acknowledge us.

There's a momentary lull – it won't last – as a taut, sinewy hand shifts gears. The stick fights him but he's more than a match. The engine bellows back, full-throated and angry.

It's Timmy, our burnt boy helper from the golf course, at the wheel – or what's left of him at least, in this demented state. What speed his legs may have lacked on the green he makes up for now as he drives the Rolls ever harder. How the tiny urchin can even reach the pedals I don't know. The boy agreed to chauffeur us… to hell?!

He throws us violently around a corner, the car veering onto two wheels. My brain pushes against my left eardrum as gravity drags me across the seat, Terrence sliding after me like a rancid joint of mutton.

Another sharp bend and momentum throws me the other way, toward the mutton-man now sucked against the far door. I reach out pleadingly with my eyeballs – it's all I can do! – but Terrence doesn't respond, doesn't even know I'm there. He's lost in the insanity of it all.

How long has it been? A handful of miles or a small eternity, I know not. My critical thinking has been immobilised.

We thunder back onto a straight. My vision begins to unravel. The passing hedgerows are a vicious snaking green; the blood in my head, my bloody head, beats in sympathy to the explosions of the straight six; my nose leaks, the inky drops curving across my lip before being whipped away into the sordid English countryside. At times we slow, but by the time I've overcome the nausea of the still natural world, we're back to it, racing through Cornwall, Devon and into Dorset; my cognisance kite-like, fluttering behind us and way up high.

Then, just as I think the final thread tying me to this mortal world is about to snap for good, the Rolls, finally, blessedly – choking on its own rage, whipped bloody by the oily demon at the wheel – BREAKS DOWN. And our ride on the thin edge of the map comes to a shuddering, merciful end. *Thank you, Lord.*

There is a moment of stillness in which I tremble before Terrence's indomitable spirit bounces forward once more.

'NOT TO WO*WW*Y,' screams Terrence, still shaking with the echoes. 'AT THE SPEEDS*TH* WE'VE BEEN GOING WE MUST BE WELL WITHIN THE HOME COUNTIES. WE'LL FIND A KINDLY LOCAL TO SHUTTLE US THE REST.'

'I SAY, BOY, HOW FAR HAVE WE COME? WHAT'S THE LAST TOWN WE PAAAAASSED?' I aim for a casual volume but come shy of the mark, my pitch breaking halfway through, my face contorting with the effort.

'We just passed Master Wright's cottage, sir,' replies the boy.

'MASTER WRIGHT? WHO THE BLOODY HELL IS HE? WHAT TOWN, YOU SIMPLETON? *HOW FAR HAVE WE COME?*' I demand.

'Town, sir? We ain't passed no town just yet. Couple of miles we've made it, I'd reckon.'

'*A couple of miles?*' I whisper, my voice collapsing.

'Don't be s*th*illy, boy,' admonishes Terrence, already settled back to his natural, balanced state. 'Couple of miles and we'd still s*th*py the bloody…'

I follow Tear's gaze across the farmers' fields that span the valley below us, swinging a left at the woodland on the far side and tracking across a gently flowing river before finally flicking my gaze to the top of a distant hill. And there, sat defiantly on the horizon, is the unmistakable outline of the country club.

* * *

We're back at the club, again. Although, really, we never left. We're not moving, no net gains, but time is still hurtling along. The horrors of our trip continue to cascade through. We're doing our utmost to put it behind us, chalk it up to experience. Our fault for hiring a child, really – they're terribly underdeveloped

We're sat in the club's lobby, doing our best to look normal. To look perfectly normal and quite respectable, thank you very much. It's not easy, because I don't *feel* normal. I feel fast. Fast and queer – my heart's racing.

Enquiries are now being made on our behalf about another motor. The club has no more to lend us, so the new plan is to borrow a patron's car along with an adult member of staff, and have them drive us to Plymouth, a mere thirty miles away, where the trains are blessedly running. The last train is at half past seven this evening. We'll take a Great Western straight to Paddington and hide out in the Horseman's Arms until Tear's due date. I know the landlord there: a discreet chap.

But the first step to success is to project an image of confidence, trustfulness. We need to appear collected and composed until some poor fool can be convinced to loan us their wheels.

But the longer I sit here in the quiet tranquillity of the club's lobby, the harder it gets. Present, it's just me, Tear, the club's receptionist, *and my thunderous bloody heartbeat*. Good Lord, I'm loud. My internals are running riot all over the serenity! The receptionist is, of course, far too polite to say anything, but I know they can hear it. Can probably bloody feel it.

'I AM SORRY,' I say, aiming for a quiet, regretful tone – but I'm still not quite on target. 'About the noise,' I whisper while tapping my chest apologetically. The receptionist assumes a confused frown, but I know they're just being polite.

'I do apologise, Mr Chalambert,' says the owner of the club, appearing behind the reception desk. He's a ratty-looking chap by the name of Mr Wheat-Whithers. Terrence doesn't respond. Doesn't move. He just sits where he is, staring dead ahead. He's assured me he's doing fine. Absolutely top notch. But it's impossible not to notice that the deep-set ring marks about his eyes from his goggles have yet to abate – if anything, they've gotten thicker. The flesh within the rings is a virulent red, while the rest of his face, the flesh outside the rings, is bone white. I look from Terrence to Wheat-Whithers and back again. Gosh, this isn't a good start. It's not a good look, certainly not a *normal* look. 'Mr Chalambert,' calls the owner. Still no response.

'Tear. Tear Bear. Terrence,' I say quietly while gently nudging him. Nothing. He's left the premises. Knowing I need to get him back at once but not wanting to startle him for fear of eliciting a too-strong response and ruining our image entirely, I do the only thing I can think of and find myself discreetly blowing on him out of the corner of my mouth. It takes a couple of gusts but Tear finally starts up again, catching the owner out the corner of his eye and playing it cool with, 'Any neeeews*th*…'

'I do apologise, sirs, but there's only one patron here,' says Mr Wheat-Whithers, 'whose car is nearby, and he requires its use, I'm afraid.'

'Double our offerings*th*. If it's more money he wants, he can have it.'

'I'm afraid he was really quite insistent, Mr Chalambert. He'll be keeping his car.'

'Well, what on earth does he need it for on a Sunday?' demands Terrence. 'There's s*th*imply nowhere to go around here.

Explain to him that it will be back from Plymouth before the day's end. He has my word, as well as my monies*th*.'

'Well, sir, if it's not too forward of me, perhaps some *coin* could bend him of his view.'

'Well, that's what I'm saying. Are you all s*th*imple out here?'

'No sir, perhaps I'm not being clear. *Real* money would carry more weight than a cheque,' says Wheat-Whithers, a condescending smile tugging the corners of his lips.

'What are you s*th*aying?' says Terrence, eyes narrowing. Wheat-Whithers doesn't answer. Doesn't look away though either. Doesn't back down. 'What is he s*th*aying, Eggy?'

'I think, Tear… I think he's saying that this gentleman is calling into repute the integrity of your coffers.'

'HOW DARE HE?' explodes Tear Bear. Whisky-soaked spit flying all over. 'Bring-me-this-impertinent-toad!'

Now, given that we're currently stranded here with nothing but fraudulent cheques and a line of credit we can't settle, one might think it sensible to let the offence slide, keep quiet and vibrate away. But when one's on a medicinal regimen as stringent as ours and still shaking from a journey that never even happened, the broader picture tends to lose itself.

'I do apologise, sir, but it is his motorcar to do with as he pleases. Perhaps I could satisfy him with half as coin and a cheque for the remainder.' This rat-faced rodent is barking up the wrong tree. We lost our last bit of coin in a wishing well… foolhardy idea, looking back.

'I shall let the offence s*th*lide,' declares Terrence, reaching for an air of magnanimity. 'I shall write *you* out the amount and you can pay him with your monies*th*.'

Ratty doesn't respond, doesn't move, doesn't blink.

'Go then, good s*th*ir. Make it so,' waves Terrence.

Ratty still doesn't move. He's more of a wolf than a rat now, and he's got our numbers. 'I'm afraid I can't do that, sir. I've already extended you a significant line of credit. But please, why not stay here an extra night as my guests, and in the morning I will personally shuttle you to the bank in Plymouth.'

'Do you dare to ques*th*tion my integrity?' Terrence whispers. He may be the prey here, but he's a big old forkful – not easy to choke down.

'Your manservant says you're broke, sir,' Ratty says softly.

'JENKINS? Don't even know him!' retorts Terrence. We have a small crowd watching now; the club's staff stand between us and the door. 'Jenkins*th*, Jenkins*th*? That his name? Wouldn't know. Know him not. Know not the man. No, lis*th*ten, he's s*th*enile. Clearly. Never laid eyes on him until he harass*th*ed me on the golf course,' fires out Terrence. He's spooked, shot back into the higher stratosphere we occupied earlier, where life really moves at speed; the speed of Tear's lips causing the beads of sweat in the creases of his jowls to shake loose and fly through the air.

Time to help the fat old bean out. Denial's the wrong tool for this job – best to let these villains know how rancid our meat really is.

'YES, HE'S BROKE. WHAT OF IT?' I roar. 'What are YOU going to do about it, sir? Cheques you have no good, not at all. Shall you send for the constabulary? Do they work on a Sunday? Suspect not, you miserable people. If Jenkins told you Mr Chalambert's spent, then surely he's told you Mr Chalambert's fortunes lie once more in LONDON. He's broke, not poor, sir. His means have slowed, not stopped.' My right hand twitches to its own beat and my eyes are having trouble focusing. But it matters little – I'm magnificent, a tornado of charisma and authority. 'Want to recuperate the credit you've foolishly extended us? Furnish us with means to travel to Plymouth. Once Mr Chalambert settles in London, he'll of course show you the full extent of his gratitude. *YOUHAVEMYWORDASAGENTLEMAN.*' I let the words hang there – nothing more to add, we've got the villains now.

'Eggy,' says Terrence, breaking the silence, 'you've wet yours*th*elf.'

* * *

'It cos*tht* me the last of my rings and my diamond-encrusted s*th*ilver aglets, but I've secured us transport, Eggy,' Tear informs me. He left to go negotiate with some marauding golfers while I dried myself off.

Regrettably, Ratty would assist us no further. Even with my speech he wouldn't be swayed. In hindsight, I should have known. His kind are too stony a people to be buoyed by charisma – better to simply whip them to market. We didn't have the whips though, and so they turned on us. We had to offer up our valuables just to get out of the club unharmed. Three gold rings from Terrence's right hand and my silver pocket watch. That covered our line of credit and then some – we are nothing if not generous – but rat-man still wasn't satisfied. He wanted us arrested. Fortunately, the noble constabulary was far too pious to work on God's Day and refused to come out. Good to see there are a few decent fellows left in this dark corner of the world.

Our near miss with the local authorities has calmed us down at least. It was the necessary dose of adrenaline needed to settle us back to an even kilter.

'I've purchased a Hansom cab and a fine-looking hors*the*. Not too shabby given the c*th*ircumst*h*tanc*the*,' continues Tear, pleased with himself. I pale as I hear it. My lips go numb and my head shrinks.

'A horse?' I say, failing to sound nonchalant.

'Yes*th*. A fine-looking stallion.'

'Come now, Tear. We're not really going to travel to London on a *horse*, are we? How very… improper,' I say, while attempting a condescending smile.

'We're not travelling *on* the hors*the*, Eggy. We're travelling in the cab; it's powered by the hors*the*. And not to London, no. We'll take the cab to Plymouth and from there the train. We'll be in London by the evening.'

'Don't be silly, old bean. A horse – such an antiquated means of transport. Listen, how about we just stay here another day. Tomorrow's Monday – the trains will be back to their usual schedule and we can shoot straight to London in comfort and class. How does that sound?'

'That's st*th*ounds bloody stupid, Eggy. We were damn lucky to get out of the club in one piec*th*e, and luckier still to not find ourselves guests of the constabulary. The sooner we get out of here, the better. If they change their minds, there are no more rings to bribe them with.' Tear holds up ten fat naked digits, bands of pale pigment denoting where his wealth once was. 'Yes*th*, a hors*th*e isn't ideal. But there's a rustic charm to it, hey, Eggy?' says Tear, trying to engender some enthusiasm.

'But… but… a horse,' is apparently the only argument I can muster.

'Good lord, Eggy, you were in The King's Own Hussars, don't tell me you're afraid of a damn hors*th*e.'

'… NO. DON'T BE RIDICULOUS,' I laugh loudly. I'm not afraid of a horse. I'm absolutely – pardon my French here – fucking *petrified* of them.

I did indeed serve in The King's Own in the war. We Brits were the only ones stupid enough to keep mounted regiments on horse-back in the midst of trench warfare. Stupidity isn't a bad thing in battle – in the chaos it's often the only thing that keeps a man alive – but I dread the cost it came at. You've not witnessed the madness of humanity until you've witnessed a horse wearing a gas mask, rear limbs blasted off by howitzers, choking on poison, as its forelegs drag it wheelbarrow-like through the sludge, unable to grasp why it can't simply stand up. They scream like men when they die, horses. A sound to make your soul ring. We beg for our mothers and sweethearts when we head off: pitiful, snivelling wrecks. Not a horse – they scream at their creator demanding only why. '*Why do I suffer?*' asks the horse, right up until that moment of profundity that it's not God but *men* that have led them off the cliff. They live for only a glimmer after that flash of self-awareness. As if true consciousness, forced into them through the agony of human conflict, is simply too heavy a thing to bear and so they burst under the burden. When St Peter greets us at the pearly gates he'll be sat atop a horse, and it's the horse who shall do the weighing: it shall know us for what we've done. And now Terrence wants to hunt down his fortune with a horse. *God* help us.

I can't tell him all this, of course. He'd think I'm mad. I'm not mad though, I'm Eggy. I look into Tear's squished, confused little eyes. Can I tell him? I think long and hard. *Can I tell him?* Tell him that they're cursed; harbingers of evil; equine portents of a road not to clip-clop down; of a race only worth racing out of?

No, of course I can't. He'd think me decidedly strange, and that's not what I want him thinking on my return to the capital. *I am not strange.* Plus, if I told him, he'd still use the bloody horse anyway.

… But I could let him go ahead, couldn't I? Meet up with him in London… but how would I explain that? Sod it, I'll just put a line under this whole thing entirely. The bank is expecting me. I should go back, like a proper banker. London was a silly idea. It's only been… years. Best to wait a little while longer.

… But would Tear Bear think me queer for the sudden change of heart, for suddenly leaving? I don't want that. What might he say back in the City? 'Eggy, the man who left for Canada for fear of a horse!' Gosh, London would be all ablaze with my name, polite society shredding the last of my shattered reputation. And where would I be? In Canada, *festering*.

Oh lordy, what's greater: my existential paranoia of horses, or my fear of missing out?

'Eggy, are you there?' asks Terrence with a frown. Lordy, how long since I last spoke?

'YES, I'M STILL HERE,' I proclaim with far too much enthusiasm, too many teeth in my painted-on smile. Panicked for time now, knowing I look stranger by the second and still not knowing what to do, I toss the proverbial shilling. It comes up tails. Heads, tails, which one's which? Before I know it, the words '*What are we waiting for hey, where's this damn horse?'* spill through my exposed pearly whites with manic gaiety.

There's a short pause in which I wait nervously, before, 'Oh, exc*th*ellent. I was starting to think you had some peculiar hors*the* problem.'

'Don't be ridiculous, Tear Bear,' I respond, following up with a good long chuckle. That should do it. I'm Egbert Whistle. Easygoing, perfectly normal, and indifferent to horses.

4

I take the reins. Terrence heaves and wriggles himself into the cab below. He offered to take charge, but the driver's seat of a Hansom cab is only built for one – and Terrence is far more than one man.

I get settled up top. Through the driver's hatch I see Tear safely securing our only piece of luggage – we've had to slim down. Our single accoutrement is a fat leather bag, filled to the brim with drink and our other essential medicines. From it I've taken a bottle of gentle tonic to calm my nerves, fortify my aura of equine indifference.

To be clear, it's not that I'm prejudiced against horses. It's that they're prejudiced against us. And well they should be. I can cross a horse in the street and a horse can cross me, I won't bat an eyelid. But it's one thing to be in the presence of beasts, and entirely another to strap on a bridle and pretend you're in charge. I wash down my fears with a quick swig of the bottle; then, with shaking hands and a flick of the wrist, I set us in motion – off to Plymouth with a horse leading us by the nose.

* * *

In spite of my best efforts to dampen the effects of our earlier hedonistic indulgences, time is still as elusive as when we were in the Rolls. I'm prepared for it this time though: I count the towns that pass, and not the minutes. Dirt paths transmute to cobbled lanes and back as stone walls narrow in dangerously before bursting out wide again, squeezing us forwards.

My eyes flit constantly between the land ahead and our four-legged chief. The pleasure of being back on the road, of watching the idyllic green countryside roll by us, is nullified by the dark-haired creature who leads us.

We circle around Truro and on through St Austell. One by one, scattered clouds evaporate from view. The sun glares down with a very un-English heat. I find the bright glare, the warm tonic, and my fearful, sullen soul are all too heavy. My eyelids begin to dip... I fight... I FIGHT... I surrender.

* * *

The first thing I'm aware of... is of being aware. Then I'm aware of a great clatter, of the world lurching sideways and of the air rushing past me. Then I'm aware of the bottle of tonic following. There is blue sky and a small bottle. Then there is no sky and a very large bottle. Then I'm unaware again. Later – a little later or a lot later I know not – I'm aware that I'm on the ground while the coach teeters over me on one wheel. I stare at it gormlessly. Then, I stare at it fearfully. Eventually, self-preservation kicks in and I stare at it warily as I scuttle backwards. I scuttle until I can scuttle no further – which isn't very far: a stone wall stands solidly behind me.

Steadied by the wall's eternal indifference, I gather my senses and begin to look – *really look* – at the scene before me. There's the lane. And there's the cab. The cab isn't in the lane. It's on the edge of a ditch to the side of the lane, teetering dangerously on one wheel. The left wheel has sunk heavily into the dirt and grass, while the right wheel spins lazily in the air. The cab isn't on its side and it's not on its bottom; it's leaning – *balancing* – on the one wheel-diagonal.

At the front, in the ditch also, still attached via twisted traces, stands the damned horse, grazing – looking for all the world as if it didn't just try to murder me.

Cautiously, I clamber to my feet and walk wide-ways to the front of this peculiar scene, making sure that our four-legged assassin can see me coming. The last thing I want to do is spook the devil.

Now, a fully functioning Eggy would be inclined to run away, to waltz with this wretched horse no more. But I'm not fully functioning; I think I'm concussed.

Keeping my distance, I climb up the ditch, past the horse, and out onto the lane. I cautiously approach the cab. I've now viewed the carriage from the totality of angles and my brain still can't fathom it: the position of our transport. So severe is the gradient at which it leans, that gravity, if not momentum, should surely have finished the job. But, quite impossibly, it remains exactly where it is, balancing on the very edge of that single wheel as if entombed in ice.

Standing on tiptoes, I peer into the passenger compartment. Tear is still in the cab, sleeping no less – warmly wrapped up in what I assume is a cosy blanket of morphine.

More astonishing than Tear's continued dormancy though, is – like the carriage – his physical position: he's in the air, perched at the very end of the bench, at its summit, directly next to the floating wheel, peacefully asleep and entirely unaffected by the laws of physics.

I watch Tear some more, unsure of what to do. I wait for reality to catch up, to send him – surely, at any moment – pitching down the bench and, in doing so, allow the cab to complete its suicidal trajectory.

But that moment never comes. Both Terrence and the cab remain as they are. Experience tells me one thing and one thing only should happen; reality tells me another. Good grief. I can only think that so substantial is Tear Bear's mass that he acts as the perfect counterpoise to the Hansom's weight, and so expansive his figure that gravity can't overcome the sticky friction between his rear and the bench.

Leaving Tear to his extraordinary magic trick, I turn my attention to how to rectify the situation. Slowly and with caution, hands held high, I inspect our steed. The harness has twisted but fortunately the traces are still fixed firmly to the shafts of the carriage. I rip out some juicy-looking grass and tentatively offer it to our leader. He stretches his neck but he can't reach.

'That's it, old bean. Grass,' I say, softly. The horse stretches again, pushing against his collar and taking up the slack. The food is still just out of reach. He leans further into his harness, stretching. And then he's stretched enough. He gives in, returning instead to easier pastures.

Disheartened but not defeated, I entice him once more, this time surrendering up a few stalks to him before backing just out of reach. The brute stretches again, more determined on this pass. The carriage groans with the slightest of forward movements – but before anything can come of it, the bastard loses interest.

I could dispense with the carrot, of course, and opt for the stick – but, one, I'm scared, and two, I can't have him wildly surging forward or else the cab, in spite of Tear's best efforts, will surely topple over with the sudden movement. No, I need our steed to come out steady. Gentle but firm. I take a swig of my tonic, brow creased in thought. And then the penny drops.

…What I need is a juicier carrot.

* * *

We're moving at a real clip now, the ditch left far behind. The suspension creaks and groans with the speed. We fly straight over another pothole and barrel round a bend. I'm holding the reins, but they're just for show at this point; our steed is gangmaster now. He was in charge before of course – I was never naïve enough to assume otherwise – but now he leads openly, having completely cast off any pretences of servitude. He turns when *he* wants to turn. Speeds up when *he* wants to speed up, and disconcertingly never seems to want to slow down. We're in luck though, for he apparently knows the way to Plymouth – I assume he's been before. Had he not known and decided to lead us elsewhere, that would have been a problem: there's no reasoning with the bugger. Fingers crossed he doesn't take a detour.

I'm still terrified of the long-faced bastard, but a touch less than before. My gift has surely ingratiated me some small degree into his good graces.

I duck as a tree branch hurtles towards me and nearly knocks my block off. Then there's a voice. I freeze. I wait. Unsure. The voice comes at me once more. "I s*th*ay, Eggy, going a bit fas*th*t aren't we?' Of course, Terrence. Thank the lord for that, for a dreaded moment I thought it was the horse. I wipe sweat from my brow and peer down through the hatch to see Tear anxiously peering up. He's finally awoken from his nap, then.

'Eggy? Bit fast, hey?' calls Terrence.

'It is fast isn't it, old sport?' I shout back over the rattle. 'Don't worry though, we'll be in good, *good* time,' I reassure.

'*W*ight, well for the sake of s*th*afety, let's slow it down a little anyway, hey? Let's just aim to a*ww*ive in moderate time,' responds Tear, doing his best to appear nonchalant.

'Sorry, can't do, Tear Bear. Our steed has the reins now.' To prove my point, I pull back heavily on the leather but our charge, if anything, speeds up. I'm beginning to wonder if we'll even stop at Plymouth. We might have to jump out as the carriage flies by. But as long as Tear jumps first to give me ample cushioning I'm sure we'll do fine.

'Now, lis*th*ten, Eg–' starts Tear, before abruptly cutting off.

I'm busy planning how to execute a successful disembarkation when I clock it. Peril in the form of an automobile materialises around the bend.

Lordy. We're on a narrow country lane, ditches and stone walls to either side. I pull quickly on the reins in the vain hope of manoeuvring us over to the edge of the road. And with these dimensions, even the edge isn't a given. It's all wasted energy, however – our steed gallops determinedly forward and right down the bullseye. The car honks at us; it, too, refusing to yield.

'Move. Clear the road. Move,' I yell but the driver doesn't budge, instead waving an arm angrily out the side, commanding *me* to move over. *I'm* not in command though.

I'm beginning to wonder if my earlier epiphany wasn't in fact a small mistake. Staring at that speeding metal block thundering towards us while our stallion thunders right back, I can't help but think I've perhaps been a touch foolhardy.

'Eggy!' cries Terrence, terrified.

The driver's honking and hand waving have now revved up to a frantic rhythm. I riposte with a wave of my own, urging *him* to be the one to move. Unfortunately, despite our mad gesticulating, neither horse nor car surrender.

Good heavens. It's a game of chicken. I'm now close enough to make out the driver's belligerent, angered expression. *Hell's bells.* Has it not dawned on this man yet? Just look at our steed for heaven's sake, man – he's clearly bloody nuts.

'Move, you thick oaf. Get out the way,' I shout.

'Eggy!' pleads Tear, busily calculating whether he can launch his fat self over the passenger door before our imminent collision. I begin to wonder the same myself. I frantically try to calculate where I'll break the fewest bones: propelling myself from the top of a speeding carriage, or *being* propelled from the top of a suddenly *not*-speeding carriage. After rounding down and carrying the one, I quickly come to the conclusion that I'm fucked either way.

I try one last time to get through to the driver. 'Move. Move, you idiot. *HE'S COKED UP! WE'VE GOT A COKED-UP HORSE,*

YOU BLOODY IMBECILE! I cry. Alas, the driver *still* doesn't submit.

With nothing more to be done, I hug my tonic and brace for impact… but it never comes. At the last moment, self-preservation finally grips the man opposite. Our souls be saved! Whether he heard me or merely looked into the manic depths of our chemically enhanced charger I don't know, but the driver rips his wheel violently to the left and careens into the ditch. We zoom past close enough to lick the paintwork. I twist around quickly to shout my thanks, only to find the man swearing at us before he's lost in a cloud of smoke and then, not long after that, lost to the distance entirely.

'What the bloody hell was that, Eggy?' squeals Tear, half petrified, half raging.

'Look, don't be cross, but he's coked up, Tear. He's a coked-up horse,' I confess through the hatch. 'We were stuck in a ditch – a real ditch, not a metaphorical one. It was a real bind, quite the puzzle, quite the head scratcher. I had to bribe the bastard out with cocaine. It's all I could think of.'

'Good Lord, you fed the hors*th*e cocaine?!'

'I regret it now, Tear Bear!'

'How much cocaine?'

'… All the cocaine.'

'All the cocaine!'

'He's a bloody horse, Tear. He weighs more than you do. The first bit didn't even touch the sides.'

'Good Lord! We've got to s*th*low him down, Eggy!' shouts Tear. He leans over the front panel and stretches a pudgy hand towards the reins, pulling down hard once he has them. But he's no more effective than I was – our steed carries resolutely onwards.

'It's no use, his mind's made up. Don't worry though, we'll jump off as we shoot past Plymouth.'

'We'll not make it to bloody Plymouth, Eggy. We've got to s*th*low him down.' Letting go of the reins, Tear casts about for a plan. He rips open our medicine chest, but before I can make out his intent I'm whipped bloody by a hail of branches – and in the assault, the tonic is torn from my grasp.

'No!' I cry, but I have little time in which to mourn as a second battery of branches comes pelting my way and I'm forced to cower for shelter. Once I'm finally in the clear, I stand to find Tear reaching over the front panel again. Light sparkles off an object in his outstretched hand. Snuggled in Tear's meaty mitt is his silver-embossed syringe, locked and loaded with a shot of morphine. With a cry, Tear brings it down hard and fast, straight into our stallion's haunch.

It's sound thinking, I guess: medicine to speed him up, medicine to slow him down. With its contents quickly expelled, Tear yanks out the syringe and holds it victoriously in the air... but the horse pays it not the slightest bit of heed, charging forward as determined as ever.

'Slow down, you stupid bloody hors*the*,' demands Tear. He turns, refilling the syringe before hammering it back down into the beast's rear; the needle plunging to the hilt before emerging once more to the sound of Tear's sweaty, grunting exertions. Still the horse displays no adverse effects.

'Plenty more where that came from, you stubborn prick!' shouts Tear, petulantly, before reloading and attacking again... and again... and *again*. 'Take that, you dumb brute,' he sneers, an arrogant, spiteful shadow settling across his visage – his ego too fragile to accept being ignored by a horse.

After what must be a dozen syringed assaults, and with Terrence's striking hand red and swollen from the repeated impact, our steed finally begins to yield. His breathing becomes ragged and his gait, no longer compass-straight, waivers uncertainly. His pace falls off to a shaky trot – but then even that proves too great an effort and he sinks to a laboured shuffle. Victory is clearly ours but Tear's too worked up to stop. Hell, he seems to be enjoying it – *the sadistic bastard* – relishing in his power over the beast, totally uncaring of the horse's certain defeat. *Somebody needs to do something.* Regrettably, I'm the only person on hand.

'Now, Tear, steady,' I call down. He pauses mid-attack.

'Don't worry, Eggy. I've got this all under control.'

'No, Tear, that's enough. He's had enough,' I call again, but Tear's committed. The syringe punctures the horse's rear to complete a baker's dozen. The added damage is immediately apparent. The horse's back left leg ceases to operate. His head dips and swings, skimming the lane, while his lolling tongue droops out the side of his mouth. Good Lord!

'No, really Tear, take it steady. *It's a horse,*' I urge, horrified. '*You'll kill him. You're going to kill him. A horse!*' My eyes begin to water and my lips tremble erratically. '*Leave it alone.*' I stretch desperately through the hatch, trying to seize Terrence's morphine-spitting fist, but the gap's too small, Terrence just out of reach. I worm harder, yearning to fit, but to no avail. Curse it! Before I know it, my hips are wedged firmly in the hatch, while up above my legs have become tangled in the reins – the sudden tension yanking our steed's head unwillingly up and back. He's a confused ragged mess, veins fit to burst all over him, but still he fights, stumbling inexorably forward.

'Just lie down. I beg of you, *lie down,*' I plead of our horse as tears run up my forehead and detach at my widow's peak. I dangle there, upside down, in a sticky web of misery. Terrence reaches for a final vial of morphine.

'*You know not what you do. It's a horse, Tear. A horse!*' I whimper.

'Yes*th*, Eggy. A dumb, beastly hors*the*,' relishes Tear. His hand is held high. The sun glints off the syringe for a final time before he thrusts down and ejaculates its potent contents into the horse's already clotted veins.

'DIE, YOU CUNT,' commands Terrence triumphantly. And with that, Julius, Julius Ceasar – I've just now named him – groans, shudders, and then falls to his knees. He courageously tries to stay there, his last stand a forlorn kneel; his body mortal, his resolve unbroken, but the momentum of the Hansom cab ploughs into his rear and he's shunted forward. The side of his face grates against the road while his giant tongue sticks to the initial point of impact and is comically, sickeningly, stretched across the distance. Julius DIES.

* * *

I stand at the head, the great big head with its great big tongue and its great big dead eyes. Terrence stands by the midriff and proceeds to give it a good swift kick. 'Yep. Definitely dead.'

'Lordy, Tear. We killed it. *We killed the horse.*'

'We did indeed, Eggy. Got a little bit carried away, in hindsight. Not to wo*ww*y though, it's only a hors*the*.'

I don't respond. I'm too damned haunted by the act we've committed. Julius, DEAD.

'I think it's a good thing. A wake-up call,' continues Tear, turning to face me. 'List*th*en, Eggy. We've had quite the ball galloping around the countrys*th*ide these last few weeks, pissing in the wind and dancing in the puddles. But it's time we put a bow on it and sent it packing. We're about to *w*eturn to polite s*thoc*t*h*iety. Time to act like gentlemen again, me thinks*th*. This hors*the* business, not gentlemanly. What we did here,' Terrence pokes Julius in the gut a few times with his foot to emphasise his point, 'was not gentlemanly at all. You can't go feeding horses*th* cocaine, Eggy.' Tear's booted nudges vibrate through Julius's loose belly, terminating in his eyes with a final, ghostly tremor, making it look for all the world like he hasn't quite left yet, like he's taking one last moment to get a good long look at us. *Lordy.*

'You didn't have to kill him though, Tear,' I say, hoarsely – no pun intended.

'No choic*the*, Eggy. A gentleman can't a*ww*ive in Plymouth on the back of a coked-up hors*the*. Best we wash our hands of the whole thing, right here.'

Tear clearly doesn't understand the magnitude of the act we've committed – and if I tried to explain it to him he'd think me deeply strange. As such, I quell the water forming in the corners of my sockets and change the subject. 'But… but how on earth do we get to Plymouth now?'

'Damn fine question, Eggy. Where are we?'

'Last sign I saw was Doddycross.'

'S*th*plendid. S*th*imply s*th*plendid,' says Terrence, turning and marching jauntily down the road.

'…Doddycross is the other way, Tear Bear. The other way.'

Tear spins on a heel. '*W*ight you are.'

5

It's a long walk back the way we've just come. The haunting image of a dead Julius stalks my every step as I trail in the wake of Terrence's nonchalant, ignorant gait. After several tobacco time-outs to catch our breath, we finally arrive outside the residence of Mr and Mrs John Bridewater. Mrs Bridewater, Eliza, is a distant cousin of Terrence's who lives on the outskirts of Doddycross.

I had remarked at the good fortune that Julius happened to die so close to a connection of Tear's, but apparently there are, 'Chalambert bastards, outcasts and ingrates s*the*eded across the entirety of the South. We Chalambert men are nothing if not fertile.'

The Bridewaters, I've been briefed, are a branch of a branch of the Chalambert family tree that only ever seemed to branch down to less fortune and further obscurity. Apparently, with no options left, Mrs Bridewater – a direct descendant of James the first, no less – had been forced to marry the – albeit successful – owner of a number of local quarries and mines. A *self-made* man. A man who had raised himself from the ranks of the working class and who found himself, in his terms, to be wealthy.

The Bridewater residence is a proud but not grand Georgian country home. Although today is a fine, hot summer's day, which always helps outward appearances. Ideally, if you truly want to get the measure of a place, it's best to do the measuring on a cold, wet January morning. That's what separates the wealthy from their poor imitations: how they handle inclement misery. Tear, however, seems to have forgotten this meteorological truth. 'He may live in a fanc*th*y house but don't forget, Eggy, that John, John the qua*ww*y man, is not one of us. Not one of me and not one of you. Not to be *tw*usted.' Like all people who were ordained with money at birth, Terrence has a healthy dislike of anyone who's accumulated theirs through toil. From Terrence's point of view, if it ain't broke, don't fix it: keep the money where it is, lest the whole house of cards tumbles down.

'Eliz*th*a, on the other hand,' continues Tear, 'was always very sweet. So sweet in fact that I petitioned daddy to intervene financially to stop her from marrying beneath herself. He beat me soundly for that suggestion,' he chuckles. 'As well he should, in hinds*th*ight. Can't help everyone, Eggy, or there'll be nothing left for anyone.'

'I'm sorry, sirs…' says the butler. He's been loitering confusedly in the doorway while Terrence stood on the doorstep and brought me up to speed on the Bridewaters, and he's finally plucked up the courage to speak.

'I'm sorry, sirs,' he repeats, 'but can I help you?'

'Yes*th*. We're here to see Mrs B*w*idewater. Eliz*th*a.'

'Are you expected, sirs?'

'Of course we're not ex*th*pected. I'd never expect to be in this ghastly corner of the world. Lead on though.'

The butler, not knowing what to do and Terrence marching confidently through the door regardless, directs us from the rear to the front parlour. In spite of our forced exercise, Tear's in high spirits; none of his enthusiasm has as of yet seeped into me, unfortunately. I'm not resting on my laurels though. I may not be able to shake off Julius and our act of equinecide just yet, but I can at least, as Tear rightly suggested, act like a gentleman. With not inconsiderable effort I've forced onto myself proper gentlemanly airs that will hopefully, with regular maintenance, last until London

– where metropolitan life will surely prove enough of a distraction that I can promptly and entirely forget about this whole cursed outing. I pride myself on my powers of selective amnesia, as any good veteran should.

'Please, take a seat, sir… I'm very sorry but who should I say has called?' enquires the man hesitantly, confusion plastered all over his face.

'Terrence Chalambert.' The butler waits for further explanation, but none comes. Eventually he leaves us to it, still none the wiser.

'Good grief,' says Terrence scornfully as he takes in the room, 'will you look at that, Eggy. He's using a creden*th*za as a bookcase.'

'Terrence,' interrupts a woman's voice, 'is that you? Is that really you?'

'ELIZ*THA*,' ra-ras Terrence boomingly, scorn turning on a penny into Etonian pomposity. 'ELIZ*THA*. Good to see you. How the devil are you?'

The way Terrence had spoken of Eliza I was expecting to find a dainty little thing, all jam and cream. Instead, I find standing in the parlour doorway a brolic badger of a woman, with fists that could crack walnuts and shoulders like anvils.

'I was not expecting this.' Eliza's voice, in contrast to her bludgeonous appearance, is high and feminine, almost childlike. 'I was not expecting this…' She pauses for a moment, a long unsettling moment; her mouth swinging freely open as she sucks Terrence in. *God, she's a weird one, isn't she?* I find myself thinking. BUT, like a gentleman, I quickly dismiss this negative impression on the grounds of my own poor judgement – I have, after all, just murdered a horse. '…not at all,' finishes Eliza.

'Quite, quite,' says Terrence, bouncing over to kiss both cheeks. 'Eliza, this is a dear friend of mine, Egbert Whis*th*tle.'

'How do you do,' I say, reserved and gentlemanly. Good job, Eggy.

'Pleasure to have you, Egbert. Now tell me, Terrence, what an earth have we done to deserve this?' asks Eliza, exhibiting entirely too much of her eyeballs. She's really making me feel weird, and I don't want to feel weird. I promised Tear I'd behave like a gentleman. Which means I must feel like a gentleman. With some effort, I take a seat and do nothing.

'Eliz*th*a, my dear, I wish I had time to *w*egale you with the story of why we're here,' says Terrence, now all pretend sorrow, 'but with time forever an enemy of us all, let us s*th*imply settle on this…' Tear lowers his voice, as if inviting Eliza into a grand secret: 'We need the means to travel to Plymouth, post has*th*e. If you can assist us on this endeavour, I shall be eternally grateful. What's more, when all is said and done, I shall reward you hands*th*omely for it. Not that you need it, clearly. Look at this place,' Terrence finishes, ingratiatingly.

'To Plymouth, you say?' Eliza simpers back.

"Fraid s*th*o.'

'Post haste, you say?'

'Indeed.'

'Post haste to Plymouth.'

'That's *w*ight.'

'You need transport?'

'Mmmhmmm.'

'You must leave this very moment to Plymouth, post haste?'

'Yesssssss*tthhhhh*,' rasps Terrence through his false smile, his patience wearing thin at the strange repetition. I decide to intervene before he says something we'll all regret. I stand and open my mouth. The room pauses. I pause too, taking a moment to compose myself, gentleman-like. I pause like a gentleman. Then I think like one. I think of a gentlemanly thing to say… But nothing immediately comes to mind. *Dash it*. I should have thought about this before standing. I've paused too long. A gentleman would never pause this long. SPEAK, EGGY. SPEAK. *Like a gentleman.*

'Is everyth-' starts Eliza. Too late, I've already committed.

'DEAD,' I proclaim mournfully, bowing my head like a – well, you know at this point –, like a gentleman.

'…Dead?' chimes Eliza in that shrill little voice.

'Yes, dead,' I continue. I've got it now, I think. 'Terrence's father, Lord Chalambert, is dead. Have you heard?'

'Dead? Your father, dead?' vibratos Eliza at Terrence, her face a picture of emotion – I wouldn't have thought she'd have cared that much.

'Did you know him?' I ask

Eliza seems taken aback by the question, upset, offended, scared. '…A little,' she slowly responds.

Curse it, Eggy, I chastise myself. I didn't expect Eliza to be so upset by the news. I reach into our medicine case and retrieve the bottle of gin. Gin cross. That'll settle her down.

'No, Eggy,' interrupts Terrence swiftly, 'no need for that.' Then, turning his attention to Eliza, 'Yes*th*, Eliza. Lord Chalambert has left us. I must return *sth*wiftly to London. The estate requires leaders*th*hip in these trying times. Do you have a motorcar, perhaps, to convey us to Plymouth?'

'…Would you like tea?'

'What?' responds Terrence, bewildered. 'No. No. I don't mean to be impolite, Eliz*th*a, but I don't want to stay for tea, or stay otherwise. Please don't take it pers*th*onally, but I want to leave. I want to get to Plymouth. Can you help?'

'…Yes, I can help.'

'Exc*th*ellent.'

'Quite.'

'Right.'

'Indeed.'

'Let's go.'

'Tally-ho.'

What on earth is going on? In many ways I feel more collected than I've been in days – Julius was a SOBERING experience – and yet the reality presented to me would suggest I'm now, more than ever, dangerously intoxicated. Is this what it's like? The natural, sober world?

'Cup of tea?' Eliza's come full circle. I'm still dining out on bewilderment when she asks this, but Terrence has transitioned.

He's about to blow his lid when a block of granite appears behind Eliza. 'John. My husband!' she proclaims, relief washing through her tone.

So, this slab of rock is John. John the husband. John the quarry owner. Good Lord, what did he quarry first – himself? You could bounce bricks off the bastard.

'John. This is Terrence. My cousin Terrence. *Terrence Chalambert,*' says Eliza, once more displaying all the eye white she can.

Right, that's it, intoxication and a dead horse or not, Eliza is definitely being odd. She said that in an odd way. But before I can decide what to do about it, the rock speaks – a sight indeed. 'Terrence Chalambert,' it says in a thick west country accent. Then it pauses. Just like Eliza, it pauses. We're all caught in a big long pause. *What the hell is wrong with these people?* I wait. I wait for somebody to do something. I'll be damned if it's me. Eventually, 'We've never had the pleasure, but Eliza has told me so much about you. John Bridewater.'

John holds out a boulder. Terrence takes it with trepidation and shakes.

'Plea*sth*ure to meet you, John,' responds Tear, examining his hand. 'I'm awfully sorry to cut this short, old bean, but as I was explaining to Eli*zth*a, my father is dead and I must travel to London post ha*sth*te. The last train from Plymouth is at seven thirty this evening. If you have a car to shuttle us the short distance to Plymouth, I will, of course, show you my appreciation as soon as I'm able.'

'A car? Aye, I have a car,' smiles John. It's fucking terrifying.

'I was just suggesting they stay for a quick cup of teeeea,' hurries Eliza, eyes still wide and weird.

'Well, of course,' says Granite John. 'Takes no more than half an hour to get to Plymouth, even by horse. You've got a few hours yet. You'll have a quick cup of tea and then I'll personally see you to Plymouth.' John still hasn't moved from the doorway. He is the doorway. Unless we dive through the window, I think we're having tea. Terrence is of the same opinion.

'Well, it appears*th* that I don't have a choice,' says Terrence pinning on a smile.

'Oh wonderful, I'll instruct William to make it so,' says Eliza, before somehow slipping through the smallest of gaps between John and the doorframe and disappearing.

'And who might you be, good sir?' asks the rock, fixing me in his earthquake.

'…Eggy,' I manage.

'Pleasure to meet you, Eggy.' It extends its boulder once more. I shake, or rather I am shook.

'You too,' I respond, utterly petrified.

There's another long, awkward silence before Terrence, unable to deny his lesser nature any longer, says: 'Lovely place you have here, John. So very, very, very… *cost*hy.'

You bastard, Terrence. Are you trying to get us crushed?! He thinks he's being subtle in his mocking condescension, but anyone who knows Terrence knows that subtlety isn't part of his repertoire. He and it are like oil and water.

'I couldn't be more pleased with it. Good old-fashioned hard work got *me* all this,' ripostes the rock, clearly aware of Terrence's poorly concealed barb.

'All this indeed… I s*th*ay, what a fine Georgian credenz*th*a I spy under all those books. How delightful,' coos Terrence in response – it's a highbrow insult though, so hopefully it's lost on John. Good grief, we can't go pissing him off – we need his car.

John locks Tear in his flinty gaze. 'Credenza, hey? Can't say that I'd know. But Eliza has a wonderful eye for these things. I reckon it takes a *woman* to know her drawers from her…*credenza.*'

Granite John and Fat Flabby Tear stare at one another with open disdain, both parties refusing to be the one to blink first. I'm slowly working up the courage to intervene before the mutual contempt boils over and strands us here, when Eliza reappears and saves me from my fortitude.

'John, darling? We're having a little problem with the tea.'

John, being – quite literally – the bigger man, breaks eye

contact first. 'Excuse me, gentlemen. I must go fix… the tea.' John bows out after Eliza.

I wait the merest of moments before turning on Terrence, 'Where the hell have you brought us, Tear? What on earth is wrong with these people?' I whisper urgently.

'He's a ghas*th*tly individual, isn't he? Did you feel his hands? I think he still work*th*s with them. He work*th*s with his hands, Eggy; for a living, Eggy!'

'I'm not talking about the bastard's hands. Eliza's no better. There is something decidedly odd here – and for once it's not us. Let's duck out while they're gone.'

* * *

I sit drinking tea. We did not escape. Terrence wouldn't budge. 'We can't leave. We need their car,' had been Terrence's excuse, and by the time I had decided that I should duck out regardless and meet him at Plymouth, William the butler was upon me, tea and biscuits in hand.

Tea hasn't proven to be the tonic for Eliza's troubles. If anything, her sickly little smile now borders on mania. In her defence, the tea is horrid. Some delightful biscuits though.

'So, how'd you have the good fortune to end up on our doorstep?' asks Granite John, the teacup lost in his giant shovels.

'Our carriage *sth*lipped a wheel,' says Terrence, draining his cup in one. His concession to me for staying is to plough through the tea as quickly as possible. Terrence reaches for the pot on the table. 'Delightful brew. You're so full of *sth*urprises down here.'

I follow Tear's lead and drain my cup too. 'Yes, delightful.'

William, finally getting into gear, waits for Terrence to finish pouring himself a fresh cup, then takes the pot and fills my cup right to the brim. Bloody fool. I carefully sip.

'That's it, drink up, gents,' encourages John, crossing his legs… and for the first time I clock it. His crossed left leg. It's not a leg at all but a wooden peg. Granite John has a wooden peg leg. How the hell did I miss that?! I immediately relax. No longer is Granite John an intimidating chunk of rock, he's a cripple. I share an internal chuckle of relief with myself. Thank goodness. There's no rationale in fearing a cripple. If a well man is ever threatened by a cripple, all one need do is break into a gentle jog. If one lacks the stamina for swift movement, no problem, locate the nearest flight of stairs, or a gentle cobbled slope, and ascend at your leisure. Threat removed.

I drain my cup. The tea tastes better.

'I see you admiring this old thing, Eggy?' says John giving his peg a friendly knock. 'A souvenir from my sea-faring days.' This big bastard on a ship? What was he, an anchor?

'Delightful. *W*eally, *w*eally delightful. Finished your tea, Eggy? Perfect. Shall we, John?' says Terrence, shutting down the conversation and standing to leave. He pushes off the sofa and no sooner has his rear left the cushion than he's careening through the coffee table, his large flabby bulk immediately shattering it and causing the legs to spit out sideways.

'Good lord,' cries Terrence, equal parts stunned and embarrassed. He spends a moment lying there, sprawled across the broken furniture, before attempting and completely failing to rise back to his feet. I guess that walk really took it out of him.

'Help me, Eggy! Help me!' puffs Tear, as he wriggles like a fat worm. I remain glued to the sofa. I'm determined to be a gentleman, and having seen Terrence debase himself like a common drunk I daren't risk standing myself. What if my legs have left for a holiday?

No, best not to risk ungentlemanly conduct. I offer him vocal support instead: 'Use your legs, Tear. Engage your legs.'

'I can't. I can't. My legs*th*. My legs*th* won't work!' squeals Tear through sweaty breaths.

'Terribly sorry about this. It must be the delayed shock – you know, his father's death,' I lie to our hosts… and as I do, I realise Eliza and John don't seem the slightest bit concerned. In fact, apart from an almost imperceptible quickening of breath from

Eliza, they haven't moved a muscle. They appear completely unfazed by Tear and the demolished table. An icy chill settles over me.

'Don't fight it, Terrence. Just relax. Just relax into it,' soothes John in a husky tone. Eliza starts to giggle quietly next to him. My icy chill intensifies.

William, like the Bridewaters, is also unfazed. Paying no notice whatsoever to the beached whale at his feet, he approaches John with a silver platter and removes the cloche to reveal what appear to be several ties: the ropey kind.

Good lord. What the hell has Terrence walked us into?! I look back down at Tear and realise that his legs *really* don't work. It's not that they're weak, but that they don't move at all. Not even a wiggle.

Eliza's giggles titillate upwards in frequency – along with my panicked heartbeat. John stands, his hard, steely glint pinned to wormy Tear Bear. 'You just relax, Terrence, and no harm will come to you.'

Mother Mary! Harm or no harm, I think Terrence may be in some trouble here. I've no idea what this is all about (though the rope leads me to believe that they're probably some kind of perverse *sexual deviants* – it would explain a lot!) but I'll be *damned* if I'm staying to find out. Clearly, this is a family matter. Time to bail. Every man for himself. I reach for the medicine case, nice and slow.

'Well, I can see you two have your hands full with Terrence here,' I announce in what I hope is a cheery tone. 'I'll leave you to it… family and all. Lovely day for a stroll. Think, think I'll walk to Plymouth–'

'I'm afraid you're not going anywhere either, Eggy,' interrupts John as he crouches down beside Terrence. 'No need to fret, though, you stay here as our guest and all will be well.'

'Yes, right. Well, tally-ho everyone. Splendid seeing you again, Terrence. Take care, old bean,' I call over my shoulder as I step carefully away from Tear's petrified form and towards the door.

'JOOOOHHHHHHNNNNNNN!' Eliza shrieks. I freeze. John looks Eliza's way. Eliza raises a shaky finger in my direction.

'Joohhhnnnn,' whispers Eliza. 'Look!'

John follows Eliza's big butch finger to its target: me.

'He's standing, John. HE'S STAAAAANDING, JOHN.' Eliza's getting worked up again. John holds out a hand to calm her.

'It's alright, Eliza. It's alright. Isn't it, Eggy? You're feeling tired aren't you, Eggy? Why don't you take the weight off?'

I've paused mid-step. Perhaps the window is a better exit at this point. Confusion flits across John's face.

'Why's he still standing, William. Why aren't they asleep yet? *What the hell's wrong with them?*' John's getting worked up as well now. Oh Lordy. I'm reassessing my advice on dealing with cripples. There are cripples and then there is Granite John.

'I don't know, sir. I made a strong brew. Perhaps it's the herbs? Perhaps they've lost their potency,' says William. Startled at the sound of William's voice so close to me, I jerk around, only to find his wrinkled old face is indeed mere inches from mine. I recoil, involuntarily stepping back – how did the old bastard get so close?! My leg bumps into the corner of the sofa and then it begins to dawn on me. I look from William to Terrence to the tea; William to Terrence to the tea… and it drops.

Villains. They've poisoned the tea.

A torrent of rage bursts forth from me – on the inside, of course. I don't want to exacerbate the worked-up rock opposite. Outside, I'm meek, but internally I'm *livid*. How dare they? No true Englishman would sink so low as to poison a guest with tea. TEA. If you can't trust the tea in this world, what can you trust?

I look at John… in a new light. This is no Englishman; no simple self-made cripple; no salt of the earth monolithic being. No. He's a savage, backwards marauder.

Summer sun cascades through the window and hits him like a prism. I see his form split. One John. One Rock. And dead centre a bearded, patched, peg-legged *pirate*. A cold-blooded blaggard. We're dealing with fucking Blackbeard here!

It's as I think this, distracted by my own internal verbosity, that William seizes the moment. Raising the silver platter high, he strikes it down hard upon my skull.

I brace for blackout… but fortunately for me, the platter crumples effortlessly around my head. HA! That'll teach the paupers. It's tin. It's a flimsy tin, pretend-silver platter. Had it been the real deal I would most certainly have joined Terrence in the horizontal position. Had we been at the house of a real gentleman right now, their fine silverware would have laid me low. Would have sunk me down. Would have splayed me…

Verbosity, Eggy. Verbosity.

That's right. Time to act. Not to think. I cast aside my gentlemanly airs and nut the old bastard in the face. Goodnight, William.

Eliza screams. Blackbeard lunges for me but Terrence – lower half still immobilised – catches John's legs in his fat hands and bites down hard.

'Wrong leg, Tear. Wrong leg!' I cry. Terrence corrects himself, releasing the wooden peg from his jaws and chomping into Blackbeard's juicy pirate calf instead. John lets out a cry.

Ha. The tables have turned, you filthy deviants! I abandon abandoning Tear and reach down for a splintered table leg to strike the rock with. As I come back up, Eliza sends me straight back down with a fist to the temple. *Christ alive that hurts.*

Meanwhile, John has managed to extricate himself from the snarling Terrence, stilling him with a vicious kick. Eliza waits, daring me to rise again.

Oh Lordy. The tables have been turned… back. That was short lived.

Taking the only sensible option left to me, I play dead. So long, Tear Bear!

'I told you to relax. IF EVERYONE JUST RELAXED, WE'D ALL BE NICE AND RELAXED BY NOW,' rages John – not at all relaxed.

Eliza's strange little giggle has returned. I peep open an eye and spy John tying Terrence up; oddly, feet first – he's not thought that through.

'What on earth is*th* the meaning of this?' squeals Terrence.

'All in good time, all in good time,' replies John, calmer now.

'Lis*th*ten. Lis*th*en. I can get you money. Lots of money. Just don't bugger me, I beg of you,' pleads Tear. John laughs. 'Lis*th*ten, lis*th*ten, how about this*th*, I'll get you money, lots of money, *and* I'll let you have your way with Eggy. How about that? How does Eggy sound? He's a handsome chap, isn't he?'

I'm torn between protesting that Terrence would make a better conquest and staying dead. I decide to stay dead. Who knows if you can even reason with sex deviants? Particularly *Cornish* sex deviants.

'We don't want your flesh, Terrence, or Eggy's there,' chuckles John. 'We do want money though. Except you won't be paying us, your sister will.'

'Tabitha? Yes*th*, yes*th* you speak to Tabitha. She'll see you right. Would you like me to speak to her? Can do. Can do. No trouble at all.'

John chuckles again. 'I don't think you're quite following. Tabitha's going to be paying that money because she's the one who put it there. There's a price on you, Terrence. *Five hundred pounds* to any family member that prevents you from attending the signing over of your dear daddy's estate.'

'That BITCH!' curses Terrence. 'I'll… I'll double it.'

'A thousand pounds?' says John sceptically – that is an awful lot of money.

'Yes*th*. That's right. I'll give you one thous*th*and pounds if you help me. Help me get to Plymouth.'

John shakes his head with a sad smile. 'No you won't, Terrence. Eliza's told me all about you. You see, we can trust your sister. But we can't trust you because you're…' John pokes Terrence with his peg. 'A. Greedy. Little. Pig.' Poke, poke, poke. 'Ain't ya, Terrence?'

'Tell you what, how about I leave you Eggy, as collate*w*al? How does that sound? I shan't let you down. I p*w*omis*the*. You have my word as a gentleman.'

John lets out his biggest laugh yet. 'You're no more of a gentleman than I. I think we'll stick with your sister. She's good for her word. Ain't she, Eliza?'

'Yes,' squeaks Eliza, 'very much so… I'm sorry, Terrence.'

'Eliz*th*a,' Terrence switches targets, 'Eliz*th*a. It's me. Te*ww*y. Te*ww*y Terrence. You can trust me, can't you?'

'No. I don't think that I can.'

With his options exhausted, Terrence breaks out into pitiful sobs, interrupted occasionally with gasps of 'You can't' and 'This is*th*n't fair'.

I continue to work on my rigor mortis as the floorboard vibrations from Tear's self-absorbed snivels wash through me. His cries and quivers begin to crescendo, and as they do the sound resonates inside me with ever more force until something unexpected, internally, shakes free: a realisation. But before I can identify exactly what the realisation is, the slippery little bugger dives away. I dive after it as it worms its way back inside me, and all of a sudden, I'm inside me too. Lordy, I've not been in here in… how long?

There! There it is! I dive further down, further in, before resurfacing with a tangled, curdled mess of *thoughts* and *feelings*. Sinking elbow-deep into the sludgy clump, I begin to parse them out. In the centre I find, coiled in fear and worriment, a shiny, wriggling *want*. I want something. I want… not to be here, playing dead on the parlour floor of a stranger's home… but that's a given… I look again, examining further. Yes. That's it… I want not to be here because… I want to be there. *Where? London.*

Yes. YES. That's my realisation. The nugget of knowledge Tear's snivelling has shaken loose. Sure, I murdered a horse and sullied my soul, but silver linings are reaped where you sow them… I'm not sure what that means, to be honest, but let's settle on this simple dictum: Julius didn't die on our way to London; Julius died so we could get to London. He's not a victim, he's a fucking martyr. Well, Julius, get to London we shall!

And these backward Cornish reprobates want to prevent that. They want to prune the freedom of me and my succulent Tear Bear. Well, let me tell you, I've not just taken out a shitting horse only to cower on Granite Pirate John's floor.

'NO, YOU BASTARDS! NO,' I cry defiantly, springing into action. I hurl the teapot at Eliza. It completely misses her. No matter, she's small fry. I kick out viciously at John's peg leg, aiming to snap it in two.

'Ow, my foot!' I cry – in pain this time. Christ. Maybe John's peg is granite as well. It's completely undamaged. Still in one piece, unlike my foot. As I hobble, John grabs me in his boulders. I struggle, but his vice-like grip only tightens further.

'I'm sorry. Have mercy. Have mercy,' I bawl pathetically. John's face turns from anger to contempt.

Yes. That's it. That's it, you salty picaroon.

I'm not a brave man, not a daring man. No, I am at heart, through and through, a coward.

The thing to be noted about a coward, however – as opposed to the fearless knight – is that the coward always considers all their options. A knight too often charges in without thought.

Now John, he's not a coward or a knight: he's a barnacled rock or a stoney pirate, depending on your currency. Either way, he's stupid. He has to be, he's working class – they've never read the classics.

And so, predictably, under the torrent of my pathetic babbling, he foolishly relaxes his grip. As he does, I reach into my jacket pocket and jab him right in the belly with a syringe packed full of morphine. How do you like them apples, John?

His shocked eyes quickly glaze over before he falls back on clouds of euphoria. The clouds aren't really real though, and he slams into the sofa, his giant size turning it to matchsticks. Terrence's fall was a big one – he's a big man – but John's actually shakes dust loose from the ceiling.

Eliza screams in horror. 'Stick a sock in it or I'll jab you too,' I warn, holding the needle out menacingly.

I'm feeling good about the situation when a cold hard object pressed to the back of my skull quickly dampens my mood. Cautiously, I turn to see William holding the largest punt-gun I have ever seen, the dangerous end pressed firmly against my cranium.

A punt-gun is an extremely large shotgun – longer than a man, at a minimum. In the days of industrialised duck slaughter, a punt-gun was affixed to a skiff and used to bring down entire flocks. You rarely see them these days owing to the fact that, one, we now prefer to slaughter *humans* in offensive quantities while applying a more sensible quota to our waterfowl, and, two, such was the enormous size of the barrels that it made drinking and shooting extremely difficult, and so the impractical, sobering cannon became obsolete.

William holds it at my head for no more than a second before its ungainly weight teeters him forward and both he and the gun collapse on the floor.

'I tried,' says William, looking up pitifully from his lowly position.

'That you did, William. That you did,' I say, trying to hide my relief at not dying. Although had he pulled the trigger, he would have certainly taken out Eliza as well.

Speaking of whom, Eliza has finally stopped screaming and is now preoccupied with hyperventilating.

'You can gasp yours*th*elf into a coma for all I care Eliz*th*a, but if you make one suspicious movement, I'll gnaw your fucking leg off, you traitorous*th* bitch!' Terrence Chalambert, ladies and gentlemen, magnanimous in victory.

'I say, William,' I say. 'What was in the tea, old bean?'

'A herb, sir. We call it Widow's Sleep round here. Not sure of its proper name.'

'And what does it do?'

'It just makes you sleep, sir. It'll make you sleep for a full day or two. I made a strong brew – on Mrs Bridewater's orders, you know,' he adds hurriedly. 'I don't know why it didn't work.'

'Terrence here, William, has an extremely efficient system. As for me, I can only assume I'm still too coked up to sleep. Is there a cure for Terrence's legs?'

William shakes his head. 'Not that I know of, sir. Apart from time.'

During my William Q & A session, Terrence, displaying a level of fitness I didn't know he possessed, has pulled himself up onto the one still-intact sofa and arranged himself into an upright sitting position. If you can ignore his oddly twisted rubber-legs, he looks relatively normal.

'Eliz*th*a,' Terrence says. Eliza pays him no heed and carries on hyperventilating.

'Eliz*th*a,' Terrence repeats. 'If you don't pay attention, I shall s*th*ee you poked full of morphine as well.'

Eliza swiftly takes a hold of herself. Shame, I think she'd rather enjoy it.

'Tabitha put you up to this, yes*th*?'

Eliza nods.

'Who els*the* has she offered money to?'

'Just about everyone, it would seem,' Eliza quavers.

'Everyone?'

'Everyone. I even heard the Coulters and the Coldwaters have banded together to find you. There was a rumour you were around these parts.'

'…Do you know why you're here, Eliz*th*a, in Cornwall with *him*?' Terrence nods in John's direction, his voice dripping with contempt.

Eliza doesn't answer.

'It's because you were happy to s*th*ettle for five hundred measly pounds. Do you know how much the inheritance is worth? Tabitha isn't rewarding you for my capture, she's s*th*pitting on you. Just like I would.'

Tears brim in Eliza's eyes.

'William. Bring the car out front,' orders Terrence.

William looks down at his feet. 'I can't, sir. It's not here. It's in the shop for repair.'

'Don't lie to me, William,' warns Terrence quietly.

'I'm not lying, sir. I promise.'

He's not lying.

'Where's the shop?' asks Tear.

'Plymouth, sir.'

'G*w*eat. That's g*w*eat.'

6

I hold a fat fleshy ankle in each hand. 'Let's go, Tear Bear.'

Terrence's dead, lead legs are by my waist. The rest of him slopes downward to the ground where he lies face down. Exhibiting more strength than one would have thought him capable of, Terrence puts a hand either side of himself and pushes his upper half off the floor. Tentatively to start with, and then with growing momentum, his hands pitter-patter forward while I follow behind with legs and feet. We proceed, wheelbarrow-like, through the lobby of the hotel and up the stairs. Our turgid circus act isn't the most inconspicuous way to move in public but *carrying* Terrence isn't an option, and I can't roll him *up*stairs. An elderly porter shuffles after us with the war chest. I was hoping there'd be a young man on hand to help me with Terrence's saggy mass, but stocks of those haven't been replenished yet – an able-bodied young man is a prize to be treasured.

I've checked us in at the Duke of Cornwall Hotel. It took hours to hitch a ride from Doddycross, and by the time we rolled into Plymouth the last train for the evening had long since rolled out. So, here we are for the night.

The Duke of Cornwall isn't terrible by provincial town standards. I had considered staying somewhere less prominent, less like me and Tear, but I figured if hordes of distant cousins really are searching for Tear Bear, they'll find us regardless of where we stay. And if I'm going to be captured, I'd rather it be in a proper bed with down pillows.

Lungs burning and with blood like porridge, we finally make it to our room. Terrence patters up to the nearest bed, and with my last ounce of strength I shove him arse-over-head. His flaccid legs splat down onto the mattress. I leave him to wrestle up his top half by himself.

'Can't apologis*the* enough about this, Eggy,' says Tear as he gets settled in. 'I do fear I've gained the odd pound or two of late.'

I dismiss the porter with a coin to keep him quiet and collapse onto my own bed, a bottle of gin in hand to quench my thirst.

'Do you believe them, Tear Bear?'

'Believe who? With what?'

'The Bridewaters. About a price being on your head. Family on the prowl.'

'Oh, it sounds t*w*ue enough alright. I should have seen it coming, t*ww*uth be told. My bitch of a sister is a canny operator, there'll be more than just family members on the prowl… But Eliz*th*a and that bastard John won't be free until tomorrow morning I shouldn't think. As long as we're on the first*th*t London train we should be ahead of the hunt.'

We left the Bridewaters and their man securely tied up in the parlour. Terrence hadn't been concerned but I didn't want them to be tied up for so long that they died; so, with that in mind, I left a note on their front door explaining their predicament to anyone who happened to come a-knocking. I also left them a saucer of milk should they get thirsty. It seemed like the decent thing to do.

'Gosh, being hunted down by your own kin. All a bit much, hey?'

'My family are a bit much. Once I get through this, I shall look at culling them. T*w*im back the dead leaves.'

'I never knew your sister had so much animosity. Surely there's enough money to go around, no?'

'It's not about the money, Eggy. It's not about her dis*th*liking me, either – although she does. It's about power. My s*thisth*ter wishes she were born a man. She's barren, you know – that's how much she despises being a woman. She believes she should be in charge, Eggy. She's never thought me capable enough to run the estates; always saw my refus*th*al to learn even the rudimentary elements of the family estate as a flaw. But what she fails to under-stand is that my steadfas*th*ht refusal to be educated is living proof of my worthiness to inherit. True nobility doesn't work for a living, their money works for them. That's entirely the point. When the rich are seen to work, they're seen to be des*th*perate. It spooks the markets. The middle classes lose faith in the top, and the lower classes get trampled as a result. At my level, s*th*imply being is the work. I work at not working. That's the c*w*oss I bear.'

'Crikey… Couldn't you offer up some money as well, to your family. Outbid Tabitha and pay off the hyenas?'

'Oh no. Just like the Bridewaters, they'd never trust me. With good reas*th*on – I'd rather choke them on my gold than share it. Fear not though, Eggy. We still have a full day and then some. Come the morning, I'll have my legs back and we shall stroll to f*w*eedom.'

'Indeed. Well, on that note, I'm going to sink this and hit the hay. Tomorrow, London. For really real this time.' I take a long draught of gin.

'…I s*th*ay,' says Terrence, 'Apologies*th* for offering you up back there to John. I would have come back for you, of course.'

'Think nothing of it. My apologies as well… for trying to abandon you. I would have come back for you too, of course,' I lie.

I lie back in bed with the gin and let the day wash over me, wash off me. Gosh, what a frightfully busy one it's been. I've packed more in today than I have in the last twelve months.

The gin quickly gets to work and as I succumb to it I drift away and dream of images of strange Cornish creatures: our little helper, the boy from the club, except he's not a boy, he is in fact a very small, hairless man, a rare gem of a human being; I see his tiny little kind stretching and then retreating across the land; I dream of Stoney John, sculpting said land – I watch him squeeze and morph; I watch pirates plunder and pillage; and then the land's a horse, Julius; he coughs, chokes and dies on the smoke and ash that drifts from the east, smothering him.

7

Monday, June 18th 1923

Morning. We're up with the worms this time, crack of dawn. Or I am, at least. Terrence's legs still don't work. If I were Terrence, I'd be a touch concerned. But I'm not Terrence, so I'm not. Neither is Terrence, even though he is Terrence. He seems completely unfazed by his paralysis. Of course, his paralysis means that I'll be doing all the work – so that might be why.

I stretch my back. Good grief, I slept terribly. I'd like to think it was due to the new room, the new bed, but I think it might in fact be Julius and that giant distended tongue of his, still weighing heavy on me. God forgive me.

I adjust my tie in an attempt to hide the stains on my only shirt. I hear a shuffling noise outside the door. I freeze. Terrence hears it too. That's good. After those strange dreams, I wasn't sure if the noise was residual.

Who the hell is creeping around at this time? Terrence passes me the poker from the fire. We've rehearsed this. The door is the only way out. The window is a fixed pane – we checked last night.

'Do it,' Terrence commands me, ready.

I fling open the door. In the dim dawn light, I make out a

shadowy figure. I grab it where its collar should be and throw it Terrence's way. The figure crashes onto the bed and Terrence quickly envelopes it in his enormous mass, smothering it entirely. I inspect the hallway for extras.

'Who are you, you vile little cretin?!' snarls Terrence.

'P-P-Paul,' says the figure named Paul.

'What are you *sth*kulking around at this hour for, Paul?'

'B-b-breakfast, sir. I brought you your breakfast. As you requested…'

Ah, yes. He's quite right. We did request that. I notice a platter and its contents scattered across the floor, my bed festooned with sprigs of thyme.

'…Yes. Sorry about that, old bean,' I say, nibbling on the crust of a rescued slice of toast.

* * *

It's a grey day outside. Matches my mood. I was just beginning to feel somewhat balanced until that unfortunate incident with our porter. I had to reassess my feelings after that. I've come to the opinion that I'm a smidge unbalanced – but no more than the world in general. I'm hoping if I lean the right way, everyone else will lean the wrong way and we'll find ourselves neutralised.

I kick a pigeon out of my way… Good God… I actually kicked a pigeon. I kicked the feathery little chap right in his breast. He didn't move for me. I assumed he would move. I wouldn't have kicked him had I known. What sign is this? Am I fast today? Or am I surrounded by really slow pigeons? This is exactly what I'm talking about: me and the world, we're out of kilter. I'm going to have to lean a little bit more to the right until the tightrope stabilises.

I hail a cab and motor across to the Royal Albert Hospital in Devonport. I'm loathe to leave my precious Tear Bear behind, but I simply can't bring him with me. And that is precisely why I'm heading to the hospital: to acquire a wheelchair.

I had Paul bring up a nice large chef's knife for Terrence before I left. I've made Tear swear that if he should be set upon by rapacious family members he'll use it, either on his assailants or on himself. He mustn't be spirited away from me. I need Terrence. I need him to come to London with me, or me with him – I don't want to go to London on my own. Plus, Julius, you know, died for *our* journey. The pair of us. May it not be in vain. Gin cross.

In addition to the knife, I also paid Paul a handsome sum to put *his* life on the line as well, should it come to it. It used to be that you could buy a man's life for a shilling and a penny, but scarcity seems to have driven up the rates. I paid Paul a whole florin, the lucky brute. Looking at my purse now though, I regret not having driven a harder bargain, convinced Paul that he was worth less. We've barely got enough coin remaining for first class and refreshments. (We relieved the Bridewaters of their purses on the way out the door but, true to form, they hadn't much to offer.)

Outside the hospital, I spy a vacant, glassy-eyed chap slumped in a wheelchair while a nurse feeds him a cigarette. Luckily, Plymouth was a hotbed of activity during the war, so there's no shortage of invalids.

'Is your name Rebecca?' I ask the nurse.

'No, Lucy.'

'That's it. Lucy. Been told to tell you trouble inside with... oh, what's his name? He's gone mad, again.'

'Michael? Was it Michael? Every bloody morning... Jake, Jake, STAY PUT,' says the nurse to dead-eyes Jake before running off inside. Mad men, ten a penny these days.

I give it a second before, 'Jake, hey? Jake!'

I wave my hand in front of his face. No response.

'Soldier! ATTEN-SHUN!' I command in my very best voice.

Jake jolts to his feet as if on strings, but, having been confined to the chair too long, his knees immediately buckle and the strings break. I catch him as he falls. As kindly as I can, I drag him over to the nearest bench, restore his cigarette and steal his chair. I pay him a quick sympathetic glance before absconding and focusing my mind elsewhere. Pays nobody nothing to dwell on these things, they're ten a penny.

* * *

I wheel Tear slowly, casually, in the direction of Millbay train station's ticket booth. Although Terrence weighs it to be more likely than not, we have no way to certify the authenticity of the Bride-waters' claims apropos bounty-hunting family members. Neverthe-less, we've let caution be our guide and I've shrouded Terrence in a large tablecloth (it was the only thing I could find sizeable enough to cover him properly). I've assured him it's done quite the trick, cast quite the illusion. But truth be told, instead of a fat dollop squeezed into a chair, he now looks like a frilly fat dollop squeezed into a chair. That's why I'm walking so damn casual. Thanks to me, they won't even notice Tear. They'll be too relaxed by my easy-going, nonchalant stride.

'Good. Gooooood,' mutters Terrence as we wheel down the pavement. 'Yeeeessss*th*. Yes*th*. Here we go. Good. Good.'

It's still quiet, the only other soul out sat on a bench a few feet from the ticket counter, lost in their morning paper.

'Yes*th*. Nice and calm. Good. Gooood. Goooooood Looooord. Good Lord. *Good Lord, Eggy*. D*w*ive by, d*w*ive by. Don't s*th*top.' Terrence is doing that thing where his lips cease to move but his voice carries on. 'About turn, Eggy. About turn.'

Carefully, casually, I spin Terrence around, not knowing why, and stroll back the way we came, attempting to whistle a jaunty tune as I go.

'Good Lord, Eggy. The woman on the bench behind the broadsheet is S*th*amantha Coldwater. Distant cousin S*th*amantha Coldwater. They're onto us, Eggy. They're onto us. We're trapped. We've walked right into their bloody, bloody trap!' This confirma-tion that Tear is indeed a hunted man has hit him hard, and he's starting to flap.

'Listen, no need to panic,' I say, surprisingly not panicking.

'Could be a coincidence. Let's leave you here.' I push Terrence into the shadow of a station column. 'I'll go back and get the tickets and we'll sneak right on the train.'

'No. Plea*sthe* Eggy, don't leave me, I beg you.' Terrence's lips still don't move – not a muscle, not a twitch.

'I'll be but a few feet away, Tear Bear.' I squeeze a fat sausage finger in each hand, so he knows I'm serious. 'Don't worry, I won't lose you.' *I wouldn't dare. Julius would be livid.*

'Don't leave me, Eggy. It's too dangerous. What if more are here?! What if John's here?'

… Lordy. I hadn't thought of that. Of *it*. Granite John the fucking pirate. *Christ alive*. What if the bugger is here? I need to hide. *It's imperative that I hide.* 'Give me your shawl,' I demand, flapping.

'What? No, it's my shawl.'

'Give me the damn shawl, Tear,' I say, grabbing the lacy corners. Terrence fights back.

'I can't. You'll expos*the* me. What on earth do you need the shawl for?'

'For a disguise. *I need a disguise*,' I flare my nostrils and pop my eyes so as to impress upon him the importance of my request.

'You don't need a disgui*sthe*, Eggy. They're not looking for you. They're looking for me.'

'What about John? What about that bastard John? What do you think he'll do if he sees me? What will happen to me, Tear? Tear?'

Terrence strokes my hair as I weep gently into his lacy lap.

'There, there, Eggy. There, there,' says Terrence comfortingly. Outclassed by my cowardice, he's forced to assume the role of leader. 'Lis*th*ten, you st*w*oll across to that ticket booth as you are. Nice and cas*thu*al. Should John appear I'll coo, like a pigeon, three times. I'll then release the brake and roll down to you, at which point you can hop on the back and we'll *w*ace to f*w*eedom. Clear?'

'You'll… you'll… coo?' I snivel back.

'Ye*sth*. Like this. Cooooo. Cooooo. Cooooo.'

I tell you what, he makes a damn fine pigeon. Almost too good.

Armed with a plan and my eyes dried off, I stroll casually, all loosey-goosey, across to the ticket booth. No one would suspect a thing.

As I wait for the ticket attendant, I hear a coo. I freeze, my ears locking onto the sound. Another coo. Lordy. Two coos. I glance back, subtle as I can, at Terrence. Was it him?

Coo. Coo! Coo? A third coo. Was it Terrence? There's no way to know, the limp git doesn't move his lips.

I'm about to bolt when a fourth coo flies on by. I spot it this time though: a pigeon pecking around the bench of Samantha Coldwater. I study it to make sure. It coos again. I relax, wiping the sweat from my eyes. That's the coo alright. That's that pigeon's coo. I wonder if it's a friend of the chap I kicked earlier, here to spook me in revenge.

It occurs to me that I've been staring at the pigeon too long. The pigeon pays me no heed, but my strange stare has caught the attention of Coldwater. I can just spot her crinkled little eyes from over the top of the paper. I try to look away from her, but I can't – I don't know what's wrong with me. I'm starting to panic.

'Sir? Sir? Can I help you, sir?'

The attendant's voice prods me from my terrified trance, and I manage to free my vision. Shakily, I spill coins onto the counter and stutter out my request. Gathering up the tickets, I arrive back at Tear just as a gaggle of ladies are preparing to enter the station. I seize the moment and coast alongside them, their large hats and thick skirts acting as the perfect shield.

Inside, I tuck Tear into another shadowy recess and let him survey the scene.

'What's the plan, Tear? Straight to the train?' I ask. Terrence doesn't answer. His focus is pinned to a queer little chap hiding behind a cloud of pipe smoke.

'That's Harry Coulter. A Coulter ins*th*ide and a Coldwater out. This is no coinc*th*idenc*the*. Eliz*th*a was telling the truth. Good Lord. Take a wide berth, Eggy. Nice and s*th*low.'

Terrence holds his breath as we pass by. I, on the other hand, breathe enough for the both of us. Frantic, shallow little breaths. Hell, I think I'm hyperventilating! We successfully skirt by Harry Coulter but I find my world growing dim. Stars twinkle in and out of view, and my legs struggle to keep up with the rolling chair. I don't want to hold Terrence up, so I give him a final push before toppling headfirst to the floor.

As I go timber, I clock that Terrence is going perhaps a touch too fast. He's picked up speed and is heading straight for the platform edge. I can't help him though, my body's too tangled up in gravity to assist.

I'm busy thinking about all this when I realise that I should be thinking about my arms. They can be awfully helpful, arms. I'm trying to remember what I need to do with them when the station floor smashes into my nose.

… I come to where I assume I landed. I see a station porter rush in and rescue Terrence from the brink, just in time. That's good, I've only been out for a moment.

The gaggle of ladies honk and flutter over to us, with people behind them also drawn to the scene. More people follow those people, oblivious to mine and Tear's antics, merely attracted by the gathering numbers. And all of a sudden, we're caught in the middle of a large and curious crowd. *Where did all these people come from?*

SHIT. Where's Harry Coulter? *SHIT.*

There! I spot him. Curiosity has made a wanderer of him, too. He's heading our way.

I surge to my feet and charge across to Tear Bear.

'Awfully sorry, ladies, good sirs. Lost this chap for a minute there. Don't mind us.' I turn Tear to the left, preparing to barge through everyone and speed away, but as I do the crowd jerks back, clearing a path before I even begin. How kind.

'Sir?' comes a lady, 'Sir! *You're bleeding.*'

'Am I?' I chuckle, seizing the moment and pushing through the gap. 'Oh dear, oh dear. Well, toodaloo!'

I glance down at my shirt. Lordy. My white shirt is a deep, deep red. I raise a hand to my nose – it's instantly drenched. Bloody Nora!

'Eggy, your nose!' says Terrence, alarmed, while I search frantically for a handkerchief. Finding one, I press it to my nose and glance behind me. The group of ladies are too polite to stare quite so obviously; Harry Coulter, however, has no such inhibitions.

'Harry Coulter, Tear. He's watching us, Tear.'

'Just get me on the train, Eggy. Jus*th*t get me on the damn t*w*ain.'

I pick up speed, heading for the first class carriage at the far end. I'm sprinting now. Casting a quick look behind me, I see that Harry Coulter, breaking into a trot, has begun to follow us.

'He's following, Tear Bear. He's following.'

'Get me on the *fucking* t*w*ain, Eggy.'

We screech to a halt outside the final door, and I realise, damn it, I realise that of course, damn it, there are steps, *damn it*, four steps up to the carriage proper. They're only small, but with this enervated sack of lard they might as well be mountains.

Terrence realises our mistake too, 'Oh, Lordy!'

Thinking fast, I back up directly from the carriage door. When I can reverse no further, I charge forward with as much speed as I can muster.

'Eggy!' screams Tear.

Tear's footrest slams into the bottom step, I push up against the chair's handles and momentum does the rest. Terrence's throne catapults him forward and his roly-poly bulk barrels straight into the train steps. Thankfully, his head clears the top step and skids along the carriage floor while his rippling midriff, like a bowl full of jelly, absorbs the main impact.

'You bas*th*tard, Eggy!'

'Good job, Tear Bear,' I congratulate. Then, sinking my hands into his amorphous mass I shove and squeeze Terrence further up the steps. He's moving, but not by much. I glance Harry's way; he's broken into full stride. Relinquishing Tear's rear, I clamber over him and pull him up from the top step. He moves a little more, but still not enough. *Curse it. We're doomed.* (Although the more I think about it, the more I think we've not thought about it: even if by some herculean display of strength I manage to drag him into the carriage proper, the train doesn't depart for another half hour.)

Harry Coulter skids to a stop in front of us – Terrence's shawl has come undone, he's horribly exposed!

'Terrence Chalambert,' says Harry, greedily.

'You keep your damn hands off me, you,' growls Terrence. Harry ignores the warning and grabs Tear by his cankles. With gravity assisting, Harry has the advantage and, in spite of me pulling frantically back, Tear begins to slide.

'I'm losing you, Tear. I can't hold,' I cry.

'Hold. You mus*th*t hold!' Tear cries back.

'Dig deep, Tear Bear. Use your legs, I know you can.'

Terrence is stretched between us like seal blubber between warring crabs.

'You can do it, Tear. I know you can. Engage your legs.'

Whether Terrence is inspired by my words or some inner fire I know not, but from deep inside him builds a feral pig-like scream. His jowls shake open, and the sound pierces me to my very core.

'Nnnnniiiiaaaaaaagggggghhhhhhhhhh,' screams Tear as his enormous thighs begin to twitch. With a mighty effort, Terrence's left leg rips free of Harry Coulter's greedy grip. His foot snatches backwards before kicking out and catching Harry right in the mouth. Harry's head snaps back and carries him to the ground where he lies unconscious.

'You did it, Tear! You did it!' I shout in wonderment.

'No time for that. We've got to go,' says Terrence, pulling himself up and testing out his new shaky legs. He takes a tentative step forward. His leg quivers, bends and begins to crumple. I move to catch him – for all the good that would do, the fat bastard – but thankfully Tear digs deep and rights himself.

'Come on, Eggy,' Tear urges again.

'… But… but the train, Tear. The train.'

'No train now. Look.'

I look down the platform. Our shenanigans have attracted some attention. A man's blowing a whistle and heading our way.

Curse it. We were so damn close.

Terrence is already waddling to the end of the platform as fast as his flimsy pins will carry him. Without so much as a by-your-leave, he turns the corner and disappears.

8

So it's true. They're really out for him. Family members and God knows who else are out coursing for my Tear Bear, my succulent pig, Terrence. Well, let's see them catch him when I'm done greasing him up. I'll grease him from head to toe, fit for a roast dinner –

'Eggy here was in America for a while. New York though, not Bos*th*ton. Weren't you, Eggy? Eggy?' A boot from Terrence shunts me from images of pork and crackling. Tear's staring at me force-fully. Oh lordy. What's wrong? Is my nose at it again? Am I drool-ing? I check my trousers – thankfully they're dry.

'I was just s*th*aying that you were in America, Eggy? Although, *now* you're in Mont*w*eal. Isn't that right, Eggy?'

'I'm in Montreal?' I look around, shocked and confused. I find I'm sat on a crate in the back of a wagon, with a pair of nuns up front driving. Relief washes over me. *I'm not in Montreal*, I think with a chuckle, *I'm in the back of a truck being chauffeured by members of the local convent. Thank god.*

'Yes. That's right. Canada. Montreal. What would you like to know?'

'No, Eggy. The S*thisth*ters*th* here were just saying that they recently visited some S*thisth*ters*th* in Boston. I mentioned you too had been that way.' Tear's eyes are boring into me something wicked. I do my best to catch up, to play it normal.

'Yes, yes, Boston. Lovely, lovely… weather. Great water. Really clean.'

'Are you sure you wouldn't like some attention, Mr Whistle?' asks one of the Sisters, the left one.

'No, S*thisth*ter Tamsyn,' jumps in Tear quickly. 'Eggy here is a f*w*equent bleeder. Nothing at all to worry about.'

How Terrence knows which nun is which, I don't know. The two look exactly alike, and not simply because they're nuns. They're of perfectly equal and exact proportions. Completely identical; from their habits (and by habits, I mean their habits, not their habits – although their garments are as matching as their mannerisms) to their height, to the pointiness of their noses, to the pitch of their voices. They are one and the same – except there's two.

This all posed a problem when I initially engaged them as I didn't know whom to address. I'm reliably informed that when dealing with nuns on the outside – that is to say, in the real world – one should always address the heaviest member of the group. Size is a form of power in the monastic world. But what should one do when confronted with a pair so faultlessly matched that the scale sits perfectly balanced… At first, I was worried I was seeing double – a brain bleed to go with my nose bleed. I held out my hands in front of me to double check I wasn't seeing double. Of course, I saw two hands – TWO HANDS – and immediately panicked. After my initial burst of fear, however, I realised that I should see two hands. I have two hands.

'TWINS?' I had then blurted out. That confused them. I had darted out in front of them, causing their wagon to come to a screeching halt, only to stand there for a while – covered in blood, with rags in my nostrils – before eventually shouting, 'TWINS?'

After escaping the train station, Tear and I had slinked and slithered carefully toward one of Plymouth's exit roads hoping to hitch another ride to, well, to anywhere really. We briefly considered heading for the docks and securing a watery passage to

London, but Tear had pointed out that if we broke down at sea, we'd surely be done for. And he's right, of course – it would have been risky. That being said, if it came to it, Terrence would make an excellent cork... but what would have been my paddle?

So, instead we had loitered in a hedgerow on the edge of town, waiting for an unsuspecting driver to pass on by. Unfortunately, we quickly realised we couldn't be certain if the passing motor vehicles were friend or foe – who knows what sorts might be out sniffing for Tear Bear! But then, as if by a miracle, what should come chugging noisily over the hill but a flatbed truck driven by a nun with a second nun in the passenger seat. *Nuns*. Surely no nuns are involved in the search, we had thought, and surely no hunter would have the impertinence, the bare-faced cheek to masquerade as a nun while on the hunt.

Not wanting to miss the moment, I sprang out in front of the nuns' wagon and grasped Lady Fortuna by the throat, at which moment I promptly froze, fretted over a potential brain bleed, and shouted, 'TWINS?'

Fortunately for me, Lady Fortuna, freed from my impotent grasp, sent Tear Bear – with the shaky legs of a newly birthed calf – tottering to the rescue. He was still wrapped in his lacy cape; his head covered in a similar manner to the nuns, tassels tickling his eyebrows. One may think that Tear's troubling appearance would only have served to compound my own poor first impression, but so alarming had been my prior performance that Tear's wibbly-wobbly, barmy comportment appeared positively normal by comparison, and with that slight gust of wind in his favour he managed to charm his way into a lift.

Nuns aren't exactly the wise and worldly sort, so they didn't even bother to ask why we needed a lift to... well, wherever they were going. Exeter, as it turns out. And before they could change their minds, we hoisted ourselves onto the back of the beaten-up old flatbed, wound our way through the crates and cargo, and took a pew right behind the cabin. The cabin's back window is missing which made it easy to engage in a bit of chitchat. Which, in turn, made it easy to keep an eye on them, just in case they do turn out to be buccaneers in disguise.

'I'm absolutely tiptop, thank you, Sister,' I say loud and direct, getting back to the present. 'Yes, I've been to Boston, wasn't there long I'm afraid. I worked in New York for a bit before relocating to Montreal.' It's true. I banked in London first, and then the bank said, 'Go bank in New York for us, will you?' and then the New York bank said, 'How about a spot of banking in Montreal?' Being the good banker that I am, I naturally said yes on all occasions. I'm not a fan of Montreal though. Everyone laughs at my French accent and the winters are frightfully long.

I'm rather tired of relocating, but at the same time it would be rather nice to relocate once more: somewhere south, somewhere less miserable. Back to England, ideally.

'What is it you do, Mr Whistle?' asks the right Sister. Sister Lowenna, I think? Yes. Lowenna's on the right. Sister Tamsyn's on the left. They're quite nice really, these nuns. They have lovely accents. They're Irish. But don't worry, Irish clergy are alright: they get a pass. It's the non-clergical Irish you have to watch out for. Particularly the young men. The poor ones. They're not good people.

'I'm a banker… I work with *mo-ney*,' I reply, stressing the word *money* while rubbing my fingers together for clarity. Who knows if these cloistered hens even know what money is?

'So, what takes you S*thisth*ters*th* to Exeter then?' interrupts Tear quickly, eyeballing me again.

'Oh, our convent is just outside of Exeter, Mr Chalambert. It's Plymouth that took us away.'

'Is that s*tho*? S*tho* what brings you to Plymouth in that case?' smiles back Tear, ingratiatingly.

'I'm sure it's not often one sees a nun behind the wheel,' chuckles the other Sister, Tamsyn, the left one, 'but Sister Lowenna here grew up driving our father's tractor. Didn't you, Lowenna?'

'Oh yes, Sister. Don't you worry, Mr Chalambert, Mr Whistle, you're in safe hands with me. I'm well versed behind the wheel.'

'Of course, we don't normally drive these days but Father Gregory is ill,' adds Sister Tamsyn.

'Yes, the Father's been awfully run down of late.'

'Bless him.'

'God bless him,' they finish in unison.

There's a pause before Tear pipes up again with, 'S*th*o, what b*w*ought you to Plymouth?'

Oh, that's right. They never answered the question. Classic Catholicism. They never get right to the point. God's always dithering, apparently.

'Wine, Mr Chalambert,' answers Sister Lowenna, finally, with a rueful laugh. 'Anything else and we'd have waited for a man to be on hand. But we can't have the diocese running dry. The congregations would surely shrink.'

'Plus, you can't leave caseloads of wine with the dockers and expect there to be any left,' tacks on the other with her own little titter.

'Wiiiiiiiiinnnnne?' Tear's interest very much piqued.

'Yes. The crates.' Sister Tamsyn nods toward the crates surrounding us. 'It's all sacramental wine. You know, for the Eucharist.'

'Yes*th*, yes*th*, yes*ttthhh*, the Eucharis*th*t.' Tear drinks in our surroundings with fresh eyes before turning to me: 'I s*th*ay Eggy, all this talk of communion has made me realise that I completely forgot to commune with my medic*th*ine… and tonic… this morning. Could you get it for me?'

'You know what, Terrence, I've just realised I, also, forgot my medicine.' I too have been overcome by a wholesome craving to suckle on something fortifying. 'But I don't have the case, you do.'

'No Eggy, that's not t*w*ue. You have it, you s*th*illy old bean.'

We loudly stare at one another; fake, pretentious smiles locked to both lips.

'*No, you do*,' I really put my jaw behind the words for emphasis.

'No, I don't,' Tear responds, not moving his lips or jaw at all.

'Yes, you do. You had the case while I pushed your chair.'

A look of horror creeps across Tear's face and is then mirrored in my own. *Bugger me silly*. We left the case in the station. Our medicine bag, our war chest… It's going to be a rough ride to London – rougher than it's already been.

'Ffffuuuuck meeeeeeeee,' the words scrape slowly out from Tear's throat.

'Excuse me?' Both heads whip back around to us.

Terrence is quick to recover, a convincing smile springing forth, his lips moving once more. 'Well, aren't we a pair of s*th*illy old goats, S*thisthers*th. We've jus*tht* realised we've left our medicine behind.'

'Oh dear, well… we could go back,' says Sister Lowenna, clearly not wanting to go back.

'No, no, no. We can't do that,' says Tear – and he's right, there's no returning to that deadly hornets' nest.

'Well, can it wait? We should be in Exeter in less than an hour. There's a wonderful chemist there, so I'm told.' That's good to know, but we've barely got enough money left to afford *third class* train tickets to London – Lord help us. There are no spare pennies left for medicinal refreshments.

Now, personally, I think I'll do alright until we get to London; my nerves are shot to ribbons but the upside of that is the buckets of adrenaline I can dine out on should I find myself needful.

Tear, on the other hand, I'm not so sure about. He's already broken into a profuse sweat and there's a tense desperation etched into the fatty creases around his eye sockets – and this is only in the knowledge that our reserves have vanished. Just wait until Father Time gets to work.

I can't speak for the cocaine, or the morphine, or the opium, or the ether, or any of the multitude of tinctures and tonics that Terrence fortifies himself with, but with regard to alcohol, be it a bottle of brown or a pitcher of claret, I would say he has a definite and heavy habit. He's not an addict, mind – he can't be, he's a gentleman, and addictions are for the poor – but a life of social sordidity has definitely inculcated in him an innate proclivity to drink, lots and often.

'Chemis*th*t, hey? In Ex*th*eter. Ex*th*cellent. Ex*th*cellent information. Yes*th*. Yes*th*. It's for our injuries, you see, sustained in the war,' says Tear, a calculating look hiding beneath an unconvincing veneer of pitiability.

'Oh, you poor things.'

'Indeed. Eggy here, filled up with s*th*hrapnel from head to toe.' That's an exaggeration. 'And my legs. Oh, what a mess – I was s*th*hot, you s*th*ee.' And that's a bare-faced lie. 'And yet here we are, having been through all that. It *w*eally is one of God's miracles*th*.'

'You sweet sirs.'

'My little lambs,' chimes the other.

'The thing is*th*…'

'Yes, Mr Chalambert?'

'… It's *w*eally a world of pain we find ourselves in if we miss our medication. You wouldn't… you wouldn't be totally aghast if we delayed the s*th*uffering with a small refres*th*hment of God's own g*w*ape?'

Well, this feels bloody awkward.

'… I don't think I follow, Mr Chalambert,' says Sister Tamsyn slowly, following entirely.

'What I mean to say is could we *veterans*… in fact Eggy here is a war hero, a war *hero*.' He really leans on the word *hero*. That one is true, sort of. I'm not a hero, I'm Eggy, but I do have a medal that says I'm a hero – a nice shiny Victoria Cross. I keep it with my toothbrush. 'Could we war heroes*th* – just to keep the old wounds at bay, the wolves from the door – could we perhaps c*w*ack open a bottle of this fine s*th*acramental wine, under God's gaze, to ease our pain for the *w*emainder of the journey?' Tear rounds off his proposal with what he hopes is a dazzling smile, having convinced himself, at least, that his speech was just the ticket. Sister Tamsyn's inscrutable gaze and Sister Lowenna's tight rigid posture would suggest otherwise.

Eventually, 'No, Mr Chalambert. I'm afraid not. I respect the instructions of your doctor in regard to your medication. But in terms of alcohol, we cannot permit it. Drinking is a sin, and a nasty one at that,' says Sister Lowenna, firmly.

We all sit there in the awkward silence for a moment before Terrence springs back up, flabbergasted, 'D*w*inking is a s*th*in?'

'Yes, Mr Chalambert. And although we reserve judgement of others over it, in our lorry I think we're entitled to enforce a little restraint.'

'I'm sure you understand,' says Sister Tamsyn with a smile, trying to soothe the rising tension.

Attempting to do the same, I throw in a smile and a word of my own. 'Of course he understands. Don't you, Tear?'

But Tear doesn't even hear me. 'I… I don't think I do understand, S*thisthtersth*… You don't app*w*ove of d*w*ink, yet you're ferrying a cartload of winc to thc parishioners in Ex*th*eter.'

The sisters take a small all-knowing chuckle, 'It's wine right now, Mr Chalambert, but by the time it gets to the lips of the parishioners it's not. You're not drinking wine, you're drinking…' Sister Tamsyn waits for Terrence to finish the sentence, but nothing comes; he just stares at them, confused and peculiar.

'… You're drinking the blood of Christ. Not wine… Christ,' Sister Lowenna finishes for Tear, with an even brighter, warmer smile on her lips, as if she were talking to a small child.

'… Ye*sttthhh*. Trans*thubsthtant*iation,' says Tear, nodding slowly, a queer look tinged with shades of disgust spreading over him in ever deeper shades.

'That's right, Mr Chalambert, so you do know.'

'Ye*sth*… I s*thuppos*the I do… I s*thay*, it's been a while since Jesus has entered me. Would you do the honours, S*thisthtersth*, perform the Eucharist, communion, the Lord's Supper?'

'Mr Chalambert, you seem to have a good grasp of the sacrament so you'll know full well that it cannot be conducted by a woman, no more than a man can give birth to a child.'

They're starting to get annoyed now with Terrence's drink-obsessed persistence. I can see the cracks forming, but I don't know what to do. Once Tear's on the scent, good luck stopping him.

'How about, Eggy? He's a man. He could knock together the c*the*remony, couldn't he?'

'Mr Chalambert, enough is enough,' shoots Sister Lowenna sharply, her patience evaporating. 'Mr Whistle here is a *banker*, not a priest.' She really pours scorn onto the word *banker*.

'No offence, Mr Whistle,' lobs the other.

'I'm not offended at all,' I lie, amicably. (I'm a little offended.)

Terrence appears to think for a moment before, 'You're quite *w*ight, S*thisth*ters*th*. I get awfully ants*th*y without my medicine. My fault. I will control myself. I shan't ask again. Perfectly imp*w*oper of me.'

Sister Lowenna relents with a forgiving smile. 'It's quite alright, Mr Chalambert. I know it must be difficult.'

Oh, well, blow me down. Turns out Tear's more of a lazy lab than a bloodhound on the scent. He's given up. That's nice to see. What a pleasant surprise. Perhaps he's turning over a new leaf. Turning for a shiny green leaf, fresh side up. He is looking a little green. I do hope we get to Exeter soon, top the old boy back up.

Pleased with the course of things, I do the only thing I can think of and watch the lush, verdant landscape chug by.

* * *

The land still chugs ponderously past me. Terrence, managing to put his cravings to one side, has reverted to norm and is taking a nap. The nuns have settled into a bubble of silence. I have an apple and a newspaper. It's a nice one, the apple; haven't read the paper yet. I've only dared to eat the skin; it went down quite smoothly though. Perhaps I shall try the flesh, see how I fare. I'll have to do it soon, mind – it's already turned quite brown. I glance between my paper and the browning nutrition. I decide to give the paper a browse first, then see where the apple's at.

We stopped off to refill the tank. It's a thirsty boy apparently, this truck. That's where I got the paper and the apple from. I don't know where the nuns got their silence from – I imagine they always have it on them. Tear went for a tinkle while we stopped off. I could have done with a tinkle myself. I didn't though. I was afraid I wouldn't be able to tinkle with the nuns nearby. *Why, it's not like nuns tinkle, is it?*

The front page of the paper is dressed up in a parliamentary sex scandal. Members of the house apparently lining up to say what a dirty little chap so-and-so is. They're all livid… that he got caught, presumably.

Having read this article countless times before, I turn the page. There's something about the Bank of England on page two. As a banker I guess I should take notice, but I don't – my attention is completely caught by the headline on page three.

Terrence Chalambert, successor to the Chalambert fortune, wanted for theft and assault.

Good lord.

I scan the article: the words *Bridewater, Arrest, Assault, Chalambert, Police* all jump out at me. I search faster, searching for the most important word of all. I'm not even reading now. My eyes bounce from top to bottom, left to right, searching.

No result. I take a breath and calm my beating heart. I read it through properly now, one word at a time, out loud to myself. I reach the end: nothing. Relief renders me into a sweet, grateful jelly. Thank heavens! There is the word *ACCOMPLICE*, twice mentioned, but both times preceded by the word *UNKNOWN.* Sweet mercy. Nowhere inked in is that dreaded moniker, that odd little name: *EGGY, EGBERT WHISTLE.*

Thank you, Lord, for making me so thoroughly unmemorable.

There's no time to bask in my good fortune, though. Information like this needs to be thrown up the chain of command as soon as possible, thereby relieving oneself of all responsibility for it. I boot Terrence awake.

'WHAT? What, what?' sputters Tear, waking up like a pantomime puppet.

'… Look.' My hand trembles trepidatiously while holding up the paper. Tear's piggy little eyes lock immediately onto it, a quiet muttering bubbling forth as he reads.

'Those bas*th*tards,' says Tear, jerking his head up, pale faced, before diving back down to the page. At the same time, his hand, as if of its own accord, stretches to his left and latches onto the lip of the nearest crate; then, as if it were nothing more substantial than a flimsy biscuit tin, rips it free. The hand creeps in through the opening before emerging back into the daylight with a shining, glistening bottle of the good stuff. His rogue appendix proceeds to raise the bottle parallel to Tear's plummy melon and pushes the top firmly into his mouth. Tear's attention, however, never leaves the page in front of him – as if his left hand were self-governing, completely independent from the rest of him. The cork and a good inch of glass are now thoroughly enveloped in his mouth, and before I even know what to make of all of this, Terrence – with nothing more than his own God-given suction power – draws out the cork, inexorably, from its tight glass sleeve, a gentle pop sounding freedom. He spits out the cork and takes a good long drink. I look on, impressed and envious.

Regrettably, the drawing of the cork and that particular, uniquely specific sound has drawn the attention of one of our hosts and a shocked, jagged gasp immediately follows in the cork's wake.

I look up as Sister Tamsyn looks down, aghast at the sight of a bottle of sacramental wine flipped almost vertical over Tear's gullet, as red drops trickle through the folds of his chins. Curiously, and quite hideously, Tear's attention is still thoroughly absorbed with the paper in front of him; his head is tilted awkwardly backward while his eyes bulge and strain to keep the article in sight.

'MR CHALAMBERT,' explodes the Sister.

'Yes*th*?' replies Tear distractedly, lowering the pacifier and peeling his eyes from the paper. The bottle is very nearly drained. He seems completely unaware of the grave sin he's just committed.

'You're *drinking*, Mr Chalambert. You're drinking the *sacramental wine*.'

'Am I?' says Tear, looking at the bottle as if noticing it for the first time. 'Well, thank you,' he adds, sincerely.

'*MR CHALAMBERT!*' rips Sister Lowenna as she hurriedly pulls the wagon over to the side and throws her support behind her sister's stunned fury.

Tear pays this second challenge not an ounce of notice, the news pulling him indefatigably back to the page. And to make matters worse, he raises the damn bottle once more and sops up the dregs. I glance at the nuns: Terrence's slurping is like a red rag to a bull. The blood drains from my face along with the last dregs of wine.

A slow whistle of rage begins to leak from the ignored nuns, like kettles on the boil. *You bastard, Terrence.* I don't know whether it's the newspaper or the baptism of bottled holy grapes that's inoculated Terrence to the glaringly obvious, but I'm hyper aware, horridly aware and somewhat terrified of the fact that we have two *very* angry nuns on our plate. I give Terrence a kick, trying to jolt him back to the land of consequence, but he doesn't even register it.

Squaring my shoulders, determined to salvage the situation, I put down my brown apple and, knock-kneed *but determined*, I wade into the furore. 'Sisters–' I squawk meekly. They roll right over me.

'*What on earth do you think you're playing at, Mr Chalambert?*' seethes Sister Tamsyn, her voice a quiet, terrifying whisper.

'Sisters–' I squawk louder this time, thinking fast of a way to rein things in. It's imperative we get to Exeter. If they boot us out here, we'll be stranded in the middle of nowhere again, only the cows for company. *What the hell is Terrence playing at?* 'Sisters, Terrence here is–' And then I stop. A hand from Terrence stops me. He looks up, looking at each Sister in turn, before looking back to the wine, then to the paper, back to the wine, before returning and settling once more on our hosts.

'Sth-sthorry,' says Tear, struggling for a moment with the word, as if it were a foreign phrase.

I follow up instantly with my pre-prepared 'Terrence here is sorry'. Then it dawns on me what Terrence has just said. He said *SORRY.* 'Terrence here is… sorry?' I ask out loud. Terrence is never sorry. That's why I was sorry for him.

'Yes*th*, Eggy. Yes*th*, S*thisth*ters,' He looks at the empty bottle in his pudgy hand with genuine regret, then at the Sisters – that look also regretful. He gives them a good long regretful look; thinking on his sorriness, presumably. 'I'm s*th*orry.'

'You're sorry?' I ask again. Double checking. Terrence is *never* sorry.

'I am, I'm s*th*orry.'

Bloody hell. He's sorry. I've never seen Terrence sorry before. Didn't know him capable… Look at him, turning over this shiny new green leaf. Gosh, I'm grinning like a Cheshire cat, like a proud parent. All my fear and anger replaced with a warm glowing pride. 'He's *sorry*, Sisters,' I beam.

'I *w*eally am ve*w*y s*th*orry,' says Tear, once more for good luck.

'You're sorry, are you?' scorns Sister Tamsyn. S*he doesn't seem to understand!*

'Yes*th*. Quite s*th*–'

'Well, sorry isn't good enough.'

'Not by half.'

'You've gone *too* far.'

'Completely unacceptable.'

'I know, I know,' says Tear, contritely, gravely. Good for him. Good for him. Regret is a healing emotion, that's what a doctor once told me.

'You've broken our trust,' says Sister Lowenna, shaking her head sorrowfully, doing what the Church does best – making one feel ashamed, embarrassed. And it's clearly working: Terrence is sorry!

As is their way the other Sister is hot on the heels of her kin: 'Abused our kindness.'

'A bridge… too far.'

'A betrayal of trust.' Alright, they're milking it a bit now.

'Actions have consequences, Mr Chalambert. You know what happens now…'

'Ye*sth*.' Terrence lets out a big regretful-sounding breath. 'Ye*sth*. I do S*thisth*ter*sth*, I do.'

'Well… on your way then, the pair of you. We shall journey with you no further. How could we? …You brought this on yourself, you know…'

Bloody hell. They're kicking us out. They're still kicking us out!

'… On-your-self,' repeats the other. 'Out you go. We can forgive but we cannot forget.'

The Sisters motion for us to leave. I don't budge an inch. I'm not getting out. There's no need to. Terrence has changed. He's changed! They'll get there, the nuns will get there too. They'll realise the miracle. *It's a bloody miracle*. A contrite, remorseful, apologetic Tear Bear. The Sisters motion again but both me and my delighted smile remain fixed firmly in place.

… To my astonishment, however, Terrence rises remorsefully to his feet. 'Ye*sth*, ye*sth*,' he sighs, before lumbering to the back of the wagon, head hung low. My lips are still spread wide in a toothy grin – I don't seem able to relax them! – but my eyes aren't smiling anymore. Rather they're flayed wide with alarm. What's happening? Why's Tear leaving? There's no need to leave. Don't get off! We can't be left here. We can't be stranded here.

THEY'LL CATCH UP, TERRENCE. THE NUNS, THEY'LL SEE WHAT I SEE. JUST GIVE THEM TIME, I want to shout – but I don't, I just sit there, bobbing slightly as Terrence dismounts, the suspension bouncing with relief.

'You too, Mr Whistle. You'll have to go too,' nods Sister Lowenna. I still don't move. I just stare up at them, a big old smile stretched across my face while my eyes start to brim with tears. *Why can't I stop smiling?!* Forcing my brain to focus, I decide that all I need to do is explain myself, the situation, the *miracle*.

Before making my supplication, I take a centring, calming breath in through my nose… and promptly choke. Or, to be more accurate, I'm stoppered just before I choke. Struggling for oxygen,

I give in on the pacifying nose breath and take in a thin, cold, raspy mouth breath that judders over my pained, beaming smile. As I do, I spot something at the bottom of my field of vision, and I realise that I've still got twisted rags stuffed in both nostrils. They stick out stiffly, like walrus tusks. *Lordy.* This won't do – I need to be taken seriously. *A miracle is a serious thing.* Using both hands, I swiftly whip out the soiled cloth – but the blood, apparently, has long ago scabbed over and they don't budge.

'Owwww,' I moan in pain – *still smiling* – unable to remove the blood-bonded rags.

The nuns – a little frightened, I think – pretend not to notice my predicament, and wave me off again with a dismissive, disdainful shake of the head.

Meanwhile, Terrence, on exiting the back of the flatbed, has turned down the driver's side, not the passenger side, and is striding towards the front of the wagon, his head no longer hung low. His steps are measured and impassive, an air of detachment draped over him. The nuns switch their attention to him, leaving me to my throbbing nostrils and tortured smile.

Terrence approaches the driver's door, his expression completely unreadable, reaches up and pulls it open. Sister Lowenna turns her head away from him as he does so, looking sternly into the distance and shaking her head. 'I don't want to hear it, Mr Chalambert.'

Terrence nods understandingly before following up with, 'Get out'. The nuns head whips back around in surprise. 'Get out,' repeats Tear, speaking with the same calm, detached demeanour with which he walked.

'Excuse me?'

'Get out.'

'Mr Chalam–'

'I s*th*aid, get out.'

'What do you think you're… What has come over you, good sir?' she stumbles, no longer sure of herself.

'This*th*. Is*th*. A. *Wobbewy*. Get out.'

Good Lord. It's a robbery? I look about me. I look at the nuns. I look at Tear. *Look at Tear.* IT'S A ROBBERY!

'E-ex-excuse me?' twitters Lowenna, frightened. Tamsyn shoots a confused, panic-stricken glance my way. I look back with a nice big smile – *I have no choice, it won't leave* – at which point, with perfectly unfortunate timing, blood begins to trickle out between rag and nostril. Tamsyn turns sheet-white.

'I s*th*aid…' Tear climbs up onto the driver's step, the wagon creaking ominously under his weight, and looks Lowenna right in her eyes, his face inches from her own, his mouth once again ceasing all movement. It's a violent, threatening air he now cuts, but his voice is still calm. 'I s*th*aid… this*th* is*th* a *w*obbe*w*y. Get out… or I'll d*w*ag you out.'

I take in my Tear Bear: hard, beady little pits where his eyes should be. He's not playing; this is the real deal. He's only gone and decided to rob a pair of nuns – the diocese even, given our cargo. *Good. Lord.*

I feel I should do something, anything, but all I can do is *smile.* So that's what I do: I smile. A big old smile is pinned across my noggin. Since I can't get rid of it, I do my best to make it a warm smile, nice and sincere. I hope they notice. *I'm trying.*

'You have to the count of th*w*ee,' says Tear in that calm tone. Utterly, utterly calm. It's terrifying. Utterly, utterly terrifying. 'Onnnnne…'

A tear runs down Lowenna's face, her previously stern judgement replaced with incomprehension. Tamsyn stares rigidly forward, a small but irrepressible tremble in her hands undermining her attempt at emotional neutrality.

'Twooooo…'

Before Tear can finish, Lowenna interrupts. 'You're scaring me, Mr Chalambert. What's going on?' she sobs quietly.

'Thre–'

Tear's minacious counting is interrupted again – this time by a quavering wail from Lowenna, followed by the juddering, mechanical rumble of the engine. She hits the accelerator and tries to speed away, but there's nothing speedy about this old thing; before she's even managed to fully depress the stiff, clanky pedal, Tear grabs her by the cowl, knotting up a good fistful of hair as he does, and, with that always-surprising burst of speed for a man his size, rips her from the driver's seat. With a cruel shove, he sends her tumbling to the road below. She stays down there, in the middle of the road, like a beaten cur, on hands and scraped knees, petrified tears streaming profusely down her cheeks, more water leaking from between her legs.

Tear pays her no heed and climbs into the driver's seat. Violence dispensed, he returns to his calm, measured movements. He turns to his passenger, Tamsyn.

'You too. Get out.'

Tamsyn nods. A whimper momentarily escapes from her throat before she catches herself and hurriedly chokes off the air. She trembles down to the ground. 'I'm st*h*orry,' states Tear once more as the nun shambles her way over to her sister in the road.

Now staring imperiously ahead, Terrence revs the engine – the nuns all but forgotten. The motor belches with smoke and before I know it, we're off, lumbering down the lane, Terrence at the wheel.

Behind us, I watch as the forlorn silhouette of a nun – a woman, a sister – stoops consolingly over her frightened and humiliated other half. The pair stay where they are, unmoving. I keep watching until the gentle curvature and the growing distance remove them from view.

I turn back to the front. My horrified smile finally begins to slip from place as the countryside trips on by. I sit a while doing nothing. I feel rather numb.

* * *

Sometime later, I know not how much later, Terrence pipes up with, 'Eggy?'

'Yes, Terrence,' I respond, quietly.

'… Are you c*w*oss*th*?'

'… Am I cross?'

'Yes*th*, are you c*woss*th?'

'Cross?'

'… Oh, you are c*woss*th, aren't you?'

'Am I?'

'Don't be c*woss*th,' Tear implores.

'Don't be cross?'

'Lis*th*hen…'

'Why would I be cross?' I laugh.

'Lis*th*hen…'

'Why would I be cross, Terrence?' I'm really cackling now. 'Why would I be cross, Terrence? What possible reason could I have for being cross?'

Terrence looks at his feet guiltily. 'Becaus*the*… becaus*the*…'

'Louder, Terrence. Clearly now,' I command, crossly.

'Becaus*the* I *w*obbed a pair of nuns,' shouts Terrence.

'NO!' I shout back. 'Because *we* robbed a pair of nuns, Terrence. *We* did.'

'Don't be s*th*illy. You didn't even lift a finger. You let me do all the work. And don't think I didn't notice.'

'That's right, Tear. I didn't do anything. *I didn't do anything.* I could have said, I should have said… Stop… but I didn't. How do you think that makes me look? It makes me look' – my mind rushes back to the paper – 'like an accomplice, Tear. The Bridewaters were one thing, that was self-defence. But robbing a pair of nuns? That's biblical, Terrence. Bloody biblical.'

'Never thought of it like that,' says Tear, quietly.

'No, that's the problem. You didn't think, did you? You didn't stop for a moment to think how robbing a pair of bloody nuns would make *me* look, make *me* feel?'

'… I'm s*th*orry.'

'You couldn't even take a single moment to think about *me*. And for what, hey? For why? Because they told you no? Because they held you to account? Because somebody for once in your spoilt fucking life told you *no?*'

'Al*w*ight. Al*w*ight. Lis*th*ten, lis*th*ten,' says Tear, sternly. 'Let's all take a breath, big, big breath… before you say something I *weg*w*et. I *w*obbed them, *I w*obbed them – are you lis*th*tening, Eggy?'

'I'm listening,' I croak, absolutely livid.

'*I w*obbed them. Not you. Me. And I won't let anyone claim differently. And before *I w*obbed them, I thought about it. I didn't think of everything, no, but I still have my reasons.' I let out a loud scoff. 'Lis*th*hen, lis*th*hen, Eggy. Are you lis*th*hening? We didn't have a choice, Eggy. It was our only option. I didn't mean to drink the wine. I promise you. It was a nervous impulse, completely invol-unta*w*y. I was in shock. Shock, Eggy. *Those damn Bridewaters*. But as soon as those nuns spotted my drink, we were done for. No coming back from that. None at all. There was no reas*th*oning with them.'

'You didn't even try. Didn't even warn me. Perhaps I could have left… for a tinkle, returned when it was safe.'

'*We didn't have time, Eggy*. I'm in the papers*th*, Eggy. *I'm in the bloody papersth.*' Terrence hammers his fist on the steering wheel, his composure slipping. 'Come the evening edition it'll be front-page news, my photo splashed all across it – my s*th*ist*h*er will make sure of that. The nuns knew my name, Eggy. Our names. Who's to say they wouldn't pick up a copy in town, put two and two together and call the police while we waited for the train? Arres*th*t is not an option, Eggy. Imprisonment is not an option. I'm in the fucking papers, Eggy. We're against the clock. Come the evening – my photo, the evening paper – everyone will know what I look like. No. Best we leave the bloody nuns back there and take this thing st*w*aight to London. We need to be off the road and s*th*oon. We need to get to London and get out of sight.'

'But they were *nuns*, Tear. You robbed a pair of nuns while I was present.'

'For their s*th*ins*th*, I'm sure.'

'You don't understand, Terrence,' I say, welling up again. 'I'm not like you. I'm not a blue-blooded bloody nobleman. I'm not a rich man, not part of the gentry. *I can go to jail.*'

'Eggy. Eggy. Take a b*w*eath. Take a big b*w*eath. You're not going anywhere because you didn't do anything. This is nothing a juicy donation won't fix. No one from the church is doing anything against you or me, do you hear? They wouldn't dare take on a Chalambert, they're as bent as we are. It would be mutual destruction.' Tear takes the end of one of the bloody nose rags still lodged in my sniffer and gently mops up my tears. 'List*th*hen, you stick with me and you'll be al*w*ight. You may not be made of gold, Eggy. But you're damn fine brass. And when you polish brass with enough elbow g*w*ease… you know what happens?'

'No.'

'It shines like gold. When I get what's owed me, I'll have enough money to buy every bucket of elbow g*w*ease in the *w*ealm. You just stick with me, Eggy. Stick with me to the signing and we'll have this all cleared up. All we need is London. Next stop, London, Eggy. London and fortune.' Tear gives the steering wheel a reassuring pat. 'I can feel it. Nothing can stop us now.'

And on that note of misplaced optimism, the wagon's engine gives a sputtering, spitting wheeze before promptly dying on us.

'… G*w*eat. That's g*w*eat.'

9

It's now essential that Tear gets to his due date safe and sound. I need him rich and powerful. I need him to make sure none of this nun business ever sees the light of day. Given last time, given how I last left London, my reputation would never survive.

Nuns! You fat bastard, Terrence!

Realising that I've once more succumbed to impotent rage, I take a swift drink of wine. Like a true friend – and a real man – I'm expending a great deal of energy repressing my rage. Bottle it up and move on. I had rather hoped the wine would have anaesthetised me of my soreness by now, but, disappointingly, it hasn't fully ironed out the creases. *Here's to trying though,* I think as I take another swig.

We're back in a train station. Numero trois. Exeter. Our stolen motor died just a few miles outside of the city proper, but our weary legs completed the journey. Terrence had advocated selling the stolen booze and using the proceeds to fund a gentleman's journey to London. I was firmly against the idea, however, stating that we had broken enough laws for one day, thank you very much. Tear's epigrammatic retort of 'In for a penny, in for a pound' had been difficult to argue with, but nonetheless common sense eventually prevailed, and we shimmied away empty-handed – well, we

took one crate with us, but only to use as barter, for essentials…
and there's a little bit for personal consumption. Alright, we did rob
some drink, but less than if I hadn't intervened.

He's not a good man, is he, my Tear Bear? Truth be told, he's
always been too rich to be anything but bad, and now that he
might be poor, it seems he can't afford to be good. That's got me
worried. I'd like to think that our journey will have no more
potholes, but should one occur I fear what Terrence might do now
he's had a taste for transgression. He is a glutton after all, a peren-
nial gourmand; he always double-dips. And what am I to do if he
does?

I take a final slurp of vino and pull my flat cap lower; we
traded the majority of our wine for workman's overalls, disguises.
Nobody's searching for Egbert Whistle of course, but a bloodied,
cravat-wearing gent walking in tow with an enormous gannet
wrapped in dirty overalls would draw attention. Best we both slum
it together. Keep quiet and stay low. If Tear's right about his sister
and the papers, come sundown the whole of London will be a
potential villain. The game is well and truly afoot.

Discarding my bottle, I approach the ticket booth.

'Alright, my cocker!' I say to the ticket clerk, in my best impression of a classless Londoner, blending seamlessly in. 'Pair of third-
class tickets to London.'

* * *

Tickets secured, I head to the platform all heavy-hipped, the very
image of a heavy-hipped tradesman, all calloused knees and
calloused… backs?… well, wherever workers get callouses.

I walk out onto the platform and cast about for Terrence – we
agreed it best if he waited here while I purchased the tickets. I spot
him halfway down – although, extraordinarily, given his frame, I
almost miss him. It seems ridiculous to think a bit of common cloth
and a woollen cap would be such effective camouflage when one is
as uniquely sized as Terrence but, I have to say, even when *I* look at

Tear, knowing full well it's him, my brain still struggles to compute. So glued, it would seem, is Terrence's appearance to gaudy wealth, so synonymous is his image with high culture that to one who knows him it's nearly incomprehensible to see him dressed as the antithesis of his breeding.

Regardless of his external appearance, Tear's internal compass, unable to be denied, has pulled him to the first-class end of the platform. I collect him and we walk down to where our tickets are valid, Terrence adopting an air of penuriousness to accompany my pretend callouses.

At the far end, we board the penultimate carriage but it's packed to the rafters with passengers. Old people. Young people. Rough people. Poor people. All the sorts of people one pays not to have to look at.

And the seats. Good grief. All crammed together. How an earth does one recline for a nap? The furniture arrangement is only made worse by the obnoxious little children that climb all over it, their feckless parents paying them no mind. Terrence and I squeeze down the aisle in search of seating – if you can call it that – continually tripping on limbs as we shuffle. Terrence's foot crunches down on the hand of a child.

'Ow, watch it, fatty!' the small brat shouts.

'Oi,' admonishes their preoccupied mother, 'that's Mr Fatty to you.'

Children from all over the carriage crow to a chorus of, 'Mr Fatty. Sorry, Mr Fatty.'

'I know I'm carrying a few Chw istmas pounds, Eggy, but Lordy these children are weally mean,' mutters Tear as we continue to shuffle. 'Once I get my money, I should have them whipped bloody. Teach them what a bit of common decthencthy looks like.'

A pair of vacant seats materialise just ahead, but they're right in the midst of the chaos.

'Let's cawwy on. Try our luck in the final one,' says Tear.

We transfer carriages. It's like night and day. Quiet. Peaceful. The odd tendril from a cigarette lazily puncturing the warm blanket of pipe smoke lingering at head height. Adults, calmly and quietly going about their lives. This is more like it. I knew they couldn't all be bad.

We proceed down the carriage. It's busy but it thins out to just one person per bench as we approach the rear. At the very end of the carriage a small maintenance closet occupies one corner, while a pair of benches facing each other occupy the other. On the bench facing the rest of the train sits a bony creature, sleeping. The bench facing bony, however, is completely free.

'I say,' I say to the withered pile. 'I say,' I say again when I get no response. It's a woman, I think, an old one. I gently tap them on the shoulder, they don't react.

'Is it dead?' I ask, turning to Terrence.

'Well, that would account for the s*th*mell,' responds Tear, disdainfully.

Now that he mentions it, there is a distinct smell down this end, hiding under the tobacco smoke. I see why there are fewer people down here now.

'Just s*th*it down, Eggy. No point standing on c*the*remony with these people,' says Tear, pushing past me and tucking himself into the corner.

'I'm not sure it's wise you taking the window seat, Tear.'

'Bes*th*t I see what's coming, Eggy. No sense in being caught blind,' replies Tear, peering suspiciously through the glass.

As I settle in beside Terrence I take a deep breath, aiming for relaxation, and realise that the peculiar smell is very much coming from the saggy hag opposite.

'Tear, *are* they dead? It *would* account for the smell.'

'S*th*cus*the* me? S*th*cus*the* me?' Terrence says assertively. No response, not a twitch. Terrence reaches forward and gives the thing a decisive flick on the cheek. Still no response. Its heavy lids remain soundly shut.

'What does it feel like?' I whisper, fascinated.

Tear reaches forward once more, giving the cheek a long, firm prod. After a while, he retracts said digit and sits back, thoughtfully.

'Clammy,' he says after some time.

A clammy old bag of bones, hey? Possibly dead. What strange little lives some people live.

We remain on the edge of our seats, nervously waiting for the train to depart. Eventually, with a shudder and a cloud of steam, the wheels begin to roll.

Oh, sweet joy. We're on our way, for really real now. Third time's a bloody charm.

* * *

'I say, Tear.' I say. We're steaming through the English countryside. It's still a lovely day; very blue and very green, but too bloody warm by half.

'Yes*th*,' responds Tear.

'What will we do when we get to London? We don't have a penny to our name.'

'Yes*th*, it's a good question, Eggy. Money will be key if we're to survive the night. Fortunately, I have had some thoughts on it.'

'Good for you, Tear.'

'Thank you. The way I see it, we need money, but we can't go to a lender because none of them t*w*ust me. We can't use f*w*iends because *we* can't t*w*ust them – can't t*w*ust them not to have been corrupted by my s*thisth*ter. And any f*w*iend who is noble enough to say nay to my s*thisth*ter's enticements is *w*egrettably noble enough to shop me into the police when they learn of me in the paper.'

'Lordy, old boy. I hadn't thought of it like that. That's quite the bind.'

'Indeed. S*tho* we need to go to someone with whom my relationship can't possibly be known of by my s*thisth*ter. But also, someone who can be convinced to look pas*tht* the papers' hurtful allegations.'

'This is quite the head scratcher.'

'Fear not, Eggy. I have just the ticket.'

'Really?' I ask excitedly, slurping on my second bottle of vino and getting comfortable, fascinated to hear what the plan may be.

'A few years ago,' whispers Tear, conspiratorially, as if around a campfire swapping secrets, 'I decided to see what money could really buy a pers*th*on. Quietly, anonymous*th*ly, I invested in a couple of g*w*oups, a couple of organisations, so as to gain *influence* with them – should such influence ever be necessary. You know, a few extra cards in my deck, a couple more strings to pull… Have you ever heard of the Six*th* Point g*w*oup, Eggy?'

'No,' I say, fascinated.

Tear looks around before leaning in close. 'They're a women's political p*w*essure group… *Feminists.*'

'Good Lord,' I gasp.

'Yes*th*. Quite. I'm their p*w*imary benefactor.'

'Say it's not so, Tear Bear.'

'"Fraid s*th*o.'

'But what do they want? They got the vote, didn't they?' I ask, confused.

'Oh, I'll be damned if I know. Give them an inch, Eggy. Still, the caus*th*e doesn't matter. It's all just good leverage to wield in parliament should the need ever a*w*is*th*e.'

'I see,' I say, reverting back to my previously fascinated form. It is fascinating, the machinations.

'Anyway, as luck should have it, they meet every Monday after-noon at Spencer House by G*w*een Park. Lady Rhondda will be good for a s*th*pot of cash. And she won't say a word. She never wanted to take my money in the first place. She'd be mortified if word got out that I was her sponsor.'

'Blow me down. You're a clever old bean, aren't you, Tear?'

'I do t*w*y.'

'Who are the others?'

'Other what?'

'The other groups you sponsor?'

'Oh, F*w*iends of the Sea, mainly.'

'Oh…'

'Quite fond of the sea… Dolphins.'

'… Right,' I say, for want of anything better. Dolphins. Who'd have thought.

Tear returns to his wine. As I do mine.

* * *

'I'll bloody well kill 'em.' says Tear, jolting me back awake. I was right on the precipice of an angsty nap.

'Kill who?'

'The Bridewaters. I'll kill 'em. I'm not talking metaphowically. How dare they go to the papers over a family matter? This is a private affair. I'm Terrence Chalambert. How *dare* they?' I glance over at Terrence as he slurs along. I'm not sure how long we've been on the train – although I note that the landscape has morphed from a verdant green to a healthy coal-smoke grey – but either way, a long while or a short while, it seems that Tear has managed to completely polish off his second bottle of wine. His eyes are bloodshot and angry.

'When I get my inhewitanc*th*e, my fortune, then we'll see how sharp these sheep's teeth *w*eally are. Let's see them take a bite out of Terrence Chalambert then.'

'Well, first you've got to get it, Tear,' I say, not wanting to engage. 'Let's get some shuteye in while we can, hey? A quick forty winks and we'll pull into the big smoke bright eyed and bushy tailed.'

'She's barren, my s*thisth*ter. A barren hag. She's spent so long wishing she were a man her womb has collaps*th*ed from neglect. No heirs. When she's done, she wants to leave it to her goddaughter. Gwendolyn. Jewel of her eye. Not even a p*w*oper Chalambert. She wants all this, all of it, just to give it away.'

'Well, fear not, Tear Bear. It shall all be yours. Probably best we get some shuteye though, hey? Put a bounce in our step.'

'Mmmm… You've killed, haven't you, Eggy?'

'What?' I ask, alarmed.

'In the war, for your medal, you must have killed people, wight?' I don't answer. One doesn't answer such a question. 'You must have, you were at…' Terrence looks at me expectantly. I don't engage. 'I need people like you, killers. I'd be a killer too if I had to be.'

Again, I don't respond. Don't even move. Best to stay still, calm as a millpond. If not, you risk stirring up the sediment, ruining the nice clean water. 'You're a good fwiend, Eggy… Whatever happens, I'll sthee you wight. Tell 'em it was all me… Not like they'd awwest you anyway, you're a bloody war hero. I love you, Eggy.'

Oblivious to the emotional tumult he's just ignited inside of me, and on that final, surprisingly tender note, Terrence leans his head back and is asleep in moments. I try to replicate but I find my angst is too much. My thoughts return inescapably to that sticky sediment.

Determined not to become trapped in a turgid melancholy, I move my mind to London. *Lovely London.* It's been almost three years since I sloped off. I'm nervous. Returning alongside Tear should help though – assuming we beat the newspapers' brewing storms. No one who matters really likes Tear of course, but he's too rich not to like to his face. Thus, everyone lives the lie that his approval is precious currency. He's a good person to arrive with, particularly for someone in my shoes.

I miss it, London. It's the bank that asked me to leave. I didn't want to go, but it's best that one does the right thing in these situations. Best that one doesn't kick up a fuss but bends politely in, to polite society. I don't like Canada. I do like London.

It's as I cautiously dream on the – as Tear would put it – *influence* I might myself be able to gain with a slice of Tear's reputation, that my second serving of sacramental grape, laced with the regular rhythm of the train, finally manages to lure me to the precipice. I'm teetering right on the brink of unconsciousness when: 'He's no friend of yours… Eggy.'

Startled, my eyes snap open as my head, jolting reflexively backwards, collides sharply with the wooden backrest. A pair of hideous, heavy-lidded, cataract-covered eyeballs consume my view; a bulbous nose decorated with whiskered warts joins in from below – the hairs close enough to stroke me.

'Jesus Christ!' I squeal, while trying to dissolve through the seatback.

'He's no friend of yours, Eggy,' the voice repeats, sounding for all the world like a cockney witch dying of miners' lung. That might sound comical – but not when it's fucking real. 'He'll use you and cast you aside, Eggy,' says the voice, as the cataracts and warts – the *face, if* you can call it that – retreat, rejoining the previously dead, mummified bone bag opposite me. Good lord. It's awake. Like a putrid mushroom gifted life.

'*What are you?!*' I whisper.

'A wise woman, Eggy,' it replies. Bony fingers appear from the folds of its rotten rags before disappearing once more into the cloth around its chest. A pipe slides out and is quickly puckered up in the saggy, melted wax that constitutes a mouth.

'You'll find no fortune with that fat fool.'

I don't respond, turning to Terrence instead. 'Tear, Tear Bear, Terrence, Terrence!' I cry hoarsely, but he doesn't respond.

'He can't hear you, Eggy. He's dead to the world.' The creature lets out a deathly cackle, expelling acrid pipe smoke in my direction. When did it light the pipe?! It continues to wheeze and heave. I watch it, whatever *it* is, not knowing what to do.

'J-Julius?' I enquire with great trepidation.

'You're friends with this,' it mocks. Reaching forward with the pucker-sucked end of the pipe, globs of spit detaching as it goes, it jabs Terrence hard in the eye.

'Owwwww.' A fat hand slaps against the wounded socket, Tear's head bowing in pain. 'Fuck me,' follows up Tear, still looking down, unaware of the dreadful ghoul hovering in front of us. 'What the bloody hell was… Good. Lord. What the hell is that,

Eggy?' Tear's wounded eyeball all but forgotten as the blood drains from his face.

'You tell me…'

Terrence, swiftly arresting his initial shock before it blossoms – like mine has – into full-blown terror, steadies himself and surges to the fore with his God-given authority. 'What are you? I s*th*ay, I s*th*ay, name yourself,' he commands.

'Terrence Chalambert,' is its gleeful reply.

'Lis*th* – Ho… how – what?' stumbles Tear, his powerful command sliding away as quickly as it slid in.

'It knows my name, too. *It knows us*,' I whisper.

'Your fortune's not for you, *Tear Bear*,' it cackles madly. 'The meek shall inherit the earth, not Terrence Chalambert. Not Terrence Chalambert.' It throws its head back and cackles louder.

'How the hell does it know us, Tear? How does it know us?' I whimper from the corner of my mouth.

Tear's as white as a sheet. 'I don't know, Eggy. I don't know.'

Bugger me silly. This is too much, too bloody much. It's fight or flight time, and internally, I've only gone and flighted. I'm still sat here, physically – physically, I'm exactly where I am – but internally I've left. Completely checked out. Terrence, next to me, he's swung the opposite way: his fists are tight, angry balls, and his wine-shot eyes are back.

'What witch*cw*aft is this,' he asks, his voice low and ominous. 'Did my s*thisth*er send you? Did my s*thisth*er send you, demon?'

'No inheritance for Terrence Chalambert,' it taunts, still laughing madly.

'You think to curs*the* me, do you? To hex*th* me? Not on my watch. Back from whenc*the* you came, you foul hag!' And before the twisted, maledicted terror can blink its milky eyes Tear's upon it; his fat fingers lost in the loose, hanging folds of skin around its neck, throttling the life from it. It wheezes and squirms as Terrence's manic shaking cracks its head repeatedly, bloodily on the hard wooden backrest. It's a terrifying otherworldly scene I gaze upon.

'Mummy, what's that man doing to Grandma?' drifts a small, boyish voice, cutting discordantly through the abominable picture I find myself party to. 'Mummy, what's happening to Grandma?' chirps the voice once more. The sound, the voice, is crystal clear. There had been a distinct deadening of the volume when my faculties fearfully checked out moments earlier and yet *this* sound, this boy's voice, sounds just like the little chap has taken a pew right in my aural cavity. I'm busy trying to marshal my few remaining wits to consider the significance of this when a sharp gasp rips past me, right on the heels of the boy's second question. The gasp is quickly echoed by my own jagged, involuntary inhale as my brain catches up. The world tunes back into full throbbing volume. The binaural rush, like sparks on tinder, triggers an immediate wave of panic, entirely drenching the previous wave of panic that caused me to vacate mentally. Too panicked now NOT to move, I turn my head, searching feverishly for the child, praying it's no more than a sick trick of my sick mind – *Oh Lord…* A few seats down, a small boy points his finger in my direction, mouth and eyes wide open. The woman whose lap he occupies is equally alarmed as she hastily wakes the man next to her. Reality barrels into me like a train at such speed I almost vomit. *Good. Lord.*

*Carpe diem*ing like my life depends on it, which it probably does, I spin back around to Terrence. 'It's not a witch, Tear. It's not a witch!' I cry. 'It's a grandma. It's a bloody grandma!'

But Terrence doesn't hear me, so subsumed is he by the crime he commits.

'Oi!' roars a voice from behind. *Fuck me.* That'll be *daddy*, I suppose.

'It's a grandma, Tear,' I cry again. 'It's a poor person's grandma!'

'It's a demon-troll, Eggy. A hellish witch,' refutes Tear, refusing to yield, gripped by a raging red mist; meanwhile, grandma's turned blue.

'No, Tear, it's a fucking grandma. She just looks like that because she's poor. She's poor and old! She must have overheard us talking. SHE OVERHEARD US TALKING!' I'm desperately trying to pry Terrence's hands from grandma's neck, but I'm also aware that to an outside eye it almost certainly looks like I'm assisting in grandma's demise.

'It's a senile old woman, Terrence. A gran–' my sentence is cut short as I find myself hurled sideways. As I sail through the air, I spy recognition finally dawning on Terrence. Then the scene slips from view as I crash into, and then through, the door of the maintenance closet. It's an almighty crash I make but, running on an expertly blended mixture of holy wine and Grade-A adrenaline, I bounce straight back to my feet – I barely feel a thing! I'm no sooner up, though, than a fist to the stomach sends me back, gasping for air. I look up and see that *daddy* has been joined by a mob of angry, rough-looking men, all champing at the bit.

'Fuckin' 'ave him, Sean,' shouts the woman with the boy.

Oh Lordy... before now, you know – and I know this isn't important, but right now it's the largest thought I can process – before now, I would never have considered *Sean* to be a name of danger. Up until this very moment, had you asked me what's the worst thing a Sean might be capable of I'd've responded that, at a push, a Sean might duck a round of drinks but certainly nothing more, nothing worse; but if you were to ask me now, right now, with tears welling in my eyes, I would say it's murder. A *Sean* is definitely capable of murder.

Mercifully though, postponing murder for a moment – or at least my murder – Sean turns contemptuously from my grown-man tears and fixes his focus on Terrence. But Terrence is quick to the fight and launches a pre-emptive strike of, 'I have money,' quickly following that up with grandma, whom he throws in the mob's direction while sliding off the bench just before they reach him. So surprising is the confidence Tear exudes behind his words, and so jarring is the juxtaposition of his privileged accent against his current attire, that the murderous Sean finds himself stopping involuntarily. Hard men at the back bump into hard men at the front as they all stagger to a halt.

'I have money,' repeats Tear, with what he hopes is an inviting smile.

'Are you alright, mum?' asks Sean of the bag of fleshy bones. It's a stupid bloody question: *Mum* is still bright blue. 'You're in for it now,' Sean says quietly to Terrence as he passes his mother gently backwards. On Sean's flanks a couple of scary-looking men crack the knuckles of thick, work-worn hands. Lordy, it's just like you read in the papers.

'I have… money,' repeats Terrence, sounding a lot less confident on this pass. The mob advances. 'I have money,' says Terrence again. I think he's broken, his mind stuck in a loop.'What's that gotta do with anything, you fucking scum?'

'Lis*th*en, lis*th*en, I'm Terrence Chalambert, I'm very important. I'm, I'm a gentleman, I'm a Lor–'

'And I'm King George. You're a fucking dead man is what you are,' growls Sean. Terrence backs up as the crowd presses forward, but quickly finds himself pressed against the rear door of the carriage. On the other side of that door is empty air, and beneath that empty air, the blurred lines of the quickly passing tracks.

As is so often the case, it appears the crowd has forgotten about me entirely. I cower in the closet. Tear's juicy form squeezed against the door has diverted all of their attention. Knowing that it shan't last long though, knowing that I shall only be spared for a time, and not knowing what these rough, manual chaps might do, how far they'd go, I decide to act. From the closet, I grab a broom by the brushy end firmly in both hands and, pushing quickly to my feet, skewer the handle right underneath old Seany boy's jaw. There's a muffled curse and a surge of activity behind him. I pay it no heed. I glance at Terrence for the briefest of moments before closing my eyes and leaping. Folding my limbs in as I take full flight, I rocket directly into Terrence's midriff, praying that its fatty composition will absorb my cannon-balling form and not simply bounce me straight back into the jaws of death. Tear has no time to move, or even flinch, before I hurtle into him. To my great relief, his gargantuan centre welcomes me in a warm embrace and, as it does, my speed merges with his weight, and physics does the rest. The door, a now-feeble opponent, bursts free of its hinges, and before anyone back on the train knows what to do, we're gliding majestically through the air: Terrence my lifejacket; the door our ship; and the air the ocean on which we sail. From Tear's warm core, I pop out my head and breathe in the freedom.

My cheesy grin and naive mood don't last long though. A door isn't a boat, and the air no buoyant liquid. With a splintering, crunching, bone-twisting crash we rejoin mother earth. The force of the impact buries me further into Tear's mass. It's pleasant at first. As I sink further in, I find myself comfortably cocooned within the inviting warmth of Terrence's epidermis. But to both of our regrets, I don't stop there. Unable to fight the forces acting upon me, I'm soon burrowed so far down that walls of flesh close in on me and the sky darkens; the world cut off by Tear's enveloping mass. From Terrence, I hear an involuntary guttural 'ugh,' before finally reaching his belly's elastic maximum, at which point it springs me flaccidly back the way I came. The door grates to a stop and Tear goes limp.

'Tear?' I ask from my foetal position as I wobble to a stop. No response. I press my ear against his chest. Nothing. I spring to my feet. *Fuck.* Below me lies Terrence, splayed across the tracks like a beached whale, his face the palest of shades, while his eyes stare lifelessly at the sky. *Good Lord.*

Then, behind Tear's possibly dead – or at the very least mortally wounded – body, I notice the train slowing to a stop. My expectation that the train would whisk our would-be punishers out of sight is – alarmingly – failing to materialise. The train should now be a distant speck on the horizon, hurtling towards the Big Smoke, but it's not. It's not a speck. It's an ever more slowly moving, very big, very close-to-me train. *Why's the bloody train stopping?!* I search around me for the answer and am greeted with a surprisingly familiar sight: Paddington Station. The train's stopping because we made it to London. We bloody well made it to London! I should feel relief, maybe even elation, at my discovery, but those sweet rewards will have to wait. The riled-up, rough-looking chaps, the abrasive commoners from the train, are disembarking from the doorless doorway at the back of the carriage.

Oh dear. Before, they looked angry, distinctly vexed, but now they look positively livid, a pack of rabid wolves encroaching on their prey. There's at least seven of the bastards working their way towards us.

'Tear?!' I cry, bending down to shake him by the collar of his overalls. There's no response. I try to heave him up, but I only succeed in raising his vacant, lolling melon and fat round shoulders an inch off terra firma before his weight tears him free from my grasp. I look fearfully between the angry mob closing in on us and limp, lifeless Tear.

'Goodbye, old bean,' I say, still completely uncertain of whether he's conked it or just conked out, but knowing there is no more time in which to ascertain an answer. Getting back to my feet, I trust the adrenaline to give me wings and begin madly sprinting down the track in the opposite direction from my would-be assassins.

As I sprint, my loose workman's overalls and the unsporting nature of my tailor-made Oxfords become tangled up in one another. Before I know it, my long majestic strides have transformed into a chaotic head-first tumble. I'm pitching straight for the tracks.

As I go, as my body, my physical self, hurtles down towards the steel rails, I find my *mind* hurtling in the opposite direction. My inner Eggy sluices out the side and spurts away. Outer Eggy, physical Eggy, watches the ground and tracks of the station coming up to meet me, but the other me – the inner me that's now outside of me – watches *mud* as it slews out under boot, blast and barrage. Confused, I blink, and in a blink my Paddington panic has completely faded out and somewhere else floods in. There's panic here, too, but it's a terrified, painful panic an order of magnitude greater than where I really am. *Oh dear.* My nice clean waters have gotten all muddied. My waters are muddied! I'm not allowed to be here. I try to leave but I can't escape. I'm suspended in motion, trapped in a bubble floating through my old haunt of *Passchendaele* in the moments before my body's impact at Paddington.

Bobbing along on top of everything, I watch a cacophony of sounds wail upon the landscape. I watch as dirt and blood and smoke and the irrepressible smell of death and shit and vomit strangle those who are too unfortunate to simply die. In front of my bubble, a carrier pigeon collides with a haphazard projectile and turns to exploding feathers.

My attention is forced beyond the shower of plumage to a line of ants down below. I watch as the line of ants, soldiers, men-made-cannon-fodder, turn and run. First one – just a boy, unable, quite literally, physically to move further forward in the torpefying sea of mud, but equally unable to remain where he is as death zips and roars by – turns. He cries for his family as he turns. Crying, he begins to wade slowly back the way he came. Another boy, much in the same way, breaks, falls apart, trembles back to a single muddled being, and flees. The peripheries of other young men begin to take note. The dam bursts and the hours of accumulated hell break through and surge inwards, soldiers left and right begin to yield, to panic, to see sense, and the immobile, stranded line of ants turns.

I hear a voice next to me, 'YOU, BOY. HAVE YOU NO SHAME? HAVE YOU NO SHAME? ABOUT TURN. ABOUT TURN.' The first boy has reached us now, all the way at the back. He doesn't stop though. Feet now on firmer ground, he speeds past us. 'YOU, BOY!' roars the voice, spit lining the bristles of its enraged, twitching moustache. The boy pays it no heed. The moustache swivels between the lone figure now behind us and the other muddied, hellish souls who have begun to encroach on the boundaries of our solid terrain. The moustache spins to and fro, frothing and fizzing as it goes. 'STOP,' it demands. But as with the first, so with the rest: its demands go unheeded. 'DESERTERS WILL BE SHOT! DESERTERS WILL BE SHOT!' cries the moustache. Then there's a crack, a drum-tearing blast right next to me – and the boy behind us, the boy in front of everyone else, drops to the ground. 'DESERTERS WILL BE SHOT,' repeats the moustache, surer now, happy at the outcome, sure of the result. The boys don't yield though. They keep coming. Towards us and soon to be past us. There's another crack and another body drops. 'FIRE, WHISTLE. FIRE,' the voice commands. 'DESERTERS WILL BE SHOT.' Then there's a Webbley Revolver in front of me, in my hand in front of me. I watch it fire and my bubble bursts and I'm colliding painfully with the tracks at Paddington Station.

In a second I'm back on my feet, my grazed knees and painful shoulder an irrelevance. The next second I'm turning around. I don't know why, but I'm turning back to Terrence. I don't know why. I should be more like those young men. *I don't know why.* I should be more steadfast like those young boys. *I DON'T KNOW WHY.* Steadfast in desertion. *I. DON'T. KNOW. WHY.* As I turn, a resolute, implacable anger spins and grows with me. It's aimed at the men that are soon to be pouncing upon Terrence. I DON'T KNOW *WHY*?! I'm crying again. I don't know why I'm angry at *those* men. They have every reason to hold me and Tear to account. But that doesn't matter to me right now. *I don't know why.*

I complete my turn, but no sooner have I taken a step forward, backwards, than Terrence, larger than life, is rushing past me in the same mad sprint to which I had attended moments earlier. His large blur doesn't stop but his face, desperately confused, does whip back my way as we once more separate: '*W*UN AWAY, EGGY. *W*UN AWAY.'

Dizzy now from pirouetting, I'm facing back the right way, which was once, maybe, the wrong way, but is now Terrence's way. I open up my stride and race alongside Tear as tears form and fall down my cheeks. 'You're alive, Terrence. You're alive!' I say, but I don't think that's why I'm crying. I DON'T KNOW WHAT'S HAPPENING.

We race one another until the platform comes to an end. Just before we reach termination Tear turns and throws himself onto the platform lip and caterpillars his way fully up. I, like a small boy playing cops and robbers, shoulder-roll up and scamper a few feet on hands and knees before surging back into my rhythm.

Behind us, the men from the train are hot on our heels; ahead, a station exit. Tear skittles through the crowd coagulating about the door, heading straight for the outside. But before Tear can make it through, a tall man, suited and booted, with a delighted, mean-spirited grin smeared across his face, materialises in front of him. '*Terrence Chalambert.*' He sticks out a foot and Terrence goes crashing to the ground. Having been surfing so closely in his slipstream I tumble down along with him. 'And Egbert Whistle, I presume.' The mean man snatches down, quick as you like, and, although his lean, angular frame doesn't seem capable – whose *would* seem capable?! – he grabs Tear by his overalls and hauls him back to his feet, the seams of his clothes about his thighs splitting and popping as he's retrieved.

Another mean-looking gentleman is quickly upon me, restraining and lifting me.

'I mean you no harm, Mr Chalambert,' says the tall one with a shit-eating grin, 'but I do have to earn a living. No hard fee–' He doesn't finish, cut off by a thunderous right hook from Sean that collides with Terrence's jaw. A second fist from a second man slams into me, into my already damaged nose. I would collapse in agony but, restrained as I am, I can't. Instead, doing all that I'm physically capable of, I cry, more.

'Oh, no you don't. He's ours,' spits Terrence's grinning captor before nutting Sean in the face. Sean drops like a sack of spuds but a third man quickly replaces him, and is presently joined by a fourth. Meanwhile, I'm caught in an abusive dance between captor and assailant, finding myself being used as shield and punching bag simultaneously. From the middle of my deadly waltz, I see that the delighted smile on the face of Tear's would-be abductor has disappeared as he tangles with an ever-increasing number of burly knuckle-swinging men.

In and amongst all this frenzied violence, the innocent disembarkees that Terrence had made to career through are desperately trying to extricate themselves from the ruckus. The mob from the train, relishing lustfully in the simple act of the brawl, have completely forgotten about me and Tear, content to sate their urges on the two strangely well-dressed boxers. Those two boxers, our jailors, the odds stacking higher and higher against them, are forced to release us as they set about an aggressive defence of themselves. In the tangle of flailing limbs and caveman-like grunts, Terrence and I manage to peel off, racing through the exit to freedom.

10

Lungs fit to burst, I peer around the corner, checking we're safe.

'Fuck me, Eggy. This is getting out of hand,' gasps Terrence through pained breaths. He's hunched over on all fours on the cobbles, gargoyle-like, paranoid malevolence spouting forth in lieu of London's acid-stained rain.

On escaping Paddington, we fled any which way the traffic was least until a deserted dead-end alley managed to lure us in and dampen our panic. The majority of passers-by fail to notice us here and those who do quickly do their utmost to ignore us. Skulking fearfully in the shadows, marred in blood and bruises, our clothing ripped and ragged, it's an alarming vignette we make.

A thick smog-infused heat blanket lies over the city. It's sweltering. Water I can ill afford to lose is evacuating my body at a dangerous rate, the blood and the sweat weighing heavily in the thick cotton of my overalls.

'Who the hell were those two men?' I croak, twisting round to look at Terrence; twisting further when my left eye fails to find focus, fixing him in my gammy right eye instead. The left side of Tear's face is swollen and bluish, like a pickled oyster slapped on the cobbles.

'It's a damn good question,' says Tear, shakily pulling out our final two cigarettes and lighting up. He hands one off to me. I cradle it gently between painful, broken lips. 'Paid professionals, I should think,' continues Terrence. 'Mercenaries, for want of a better word. My bitch of a s*this*t*h*ter's *w*eally gone to town on this…'

Good heavens, this really is getting out of hand. My mind skitters over the patchwork of horrors we've suffered: Julius; the Bridewaters; the train station; the nuns; a grandma – a fucking *grandma*; and now… Passchendaele. And all since… when? Yesterday. Yesterday?! Good lord. No more!

Blood splashes onto the paper of my cigarette as I watch a diseased-looking rat take a wide berth around us and scurry down the alley. I raise a sleeve gently to my nose but on contact my whole head splinters in pain and flinches away, tilting my gaze upwards where a sunbeam bouncing off the smashed glass of a broken window lances me straight in my tender eyes, causing them to water, the water in turn corroding painfully as it catches in the split skin of my right cheek.

'Owwww,' I mew wretchedly, wanting to cry more but knowing that will only make me… cry more.

'Come on, old bean. We can't hang about here for too long. Help me up,' says Tear, completely oblivious to my suffering.

I don't move. Don't respond.

'Eggy. Help me up will you.'

I still don't move. Not a muscle.

'Eggy?'

'I'M GOING FOR A TINKLE.' And without so much as a backward look I stride to the alley's exit, to the sunshine, to London waiting just beyond.

'Eggy…'

'I'M GOING FOR A TINKLE. GOODBYE, TERRENCE,' I proclaim once more, letting anger be the scaffold to my resolve. I approach the alley exit, the threshold through which freedom lies.

'No. You're not, Eggy.'

'YES, I BLOODY WELL AM,' I call back hysterically, pausing right on the line.

'No, you're not, Eggy,' says Tear once more, calmly. Why's he so damn calm?

'I'M NOT?' I ask, turning back around, attempting to stay determined, defiant; attempting to hide my sudden doubt, my sudden uncertainty; and failing miserably at all of the above.

'They knew your name, Eggy.'

'… W-What?'

'The men at the station, Eggy. The men my s*thisth*ter sent. The two men at the station who g*w*abbed us…'

'The two men… in the knock-off Savile Row suits?' I whisper.

'Ye*sth*.'

'The two men… in the second-hand brogues?' I follow up.

'Indeed.'

'The two men… with the poorly attended stubble and the obnoxious fragrance?' I don't know why it's important to be so specific, but it is. It simply is. I feel a great sense of unease stirring inside me. There's a quiet, menacing hostility projecting from Tear… at me. It's being projected at *me*.

'That's them,' says Tear, very softly. 'They knew your name, Eggy.'

'What?'

'They knew your name, Eggy. Egbert Whistle… That's what they said… Egbert Whistle, I presume.'

Fucking hell. He's right. The well-dressed villain that arrested Tear, he knew my bloody name.

'You've been comp*w*omised, Eggy. They know who you are. They know you're with me. My s*thisth*ter's on the hunt for you too, Eggy. And should you leave, and should my s*thisth*ter get you, you'd be in g*w*ave danger, Eggy.'

'What? Why?'

'For one, because you opposed her, Eggy. You picked a side, and it wasn't hers. She's a s*th*piteful bitch. And for two, because my s*thisth*ter will want to know where I am, Eggy. She'll want you to tell her.'

'But I won't know,' I riposte hastily. And then, even more hastily, 'If I leave, w-which I'm not… leaving. But if I did, I wouldn't know where you are. I'd tell her… I'd tell her I don't know, because I don't know.' I don't feel well.

'Eggy. Eggy. Eggy,' says Tear, gently – almost pityingly, almost scornfully. He's still squatting like a gargoyle on the piss-slick ground, his bruised face cast in malicious shadow. 'She'd never believe you. You've come this far with me. Why would you turn now? No. And even if she did believe you, she'd want to make sure. Find out what my plans are. Do you know how she'd make sure, Eggy? She'd hurt you. She'd *w*eally, *w*eally hurt you. Torture. Jus*tht* to make sure you're telling the truth. Do you know how I know, Eggy?'

I give a small, frightened shake.

'Because it's exactly what I'd do. Why not? Bes*tht* to dot the Is and cross the Ts, hey? Who cares if a few Eggys get cracked along the way? This isn't a game. For my s*thisth*ter, maybe. But not for you. You can't afford to play it.'

… Fucking hell. What the fucking hell have I got myself mixed up in…?

'Now, help me up, old bean.'

I feel a numbness creep over me. When it's done, and I'm fully enswathed, I hold out a hand for Tear, timidly asking, 'To see this Six Point Group?'

Terrence responds with a small, haunting chuckle, still perched on his haunches, leaving my hand outstretched, quivering in mid-air. 'Tell me, Eggy, given the lengths my s*thisth*er has gone to thus far, what you think the chances are of us being able to simply st*w*oll through Lincoln's Inn Fields tomorrow and walk straight through the office door?'

Now that Tear mentions it, that does seem rather unlikely. After all, the simplest way to find Tear and stop him is to have him picked up at the one place you know he has to be.

Good. Bloody. Lord. What the hell *have I* got myself mixed up in?

'No, Eggy. No Six Point Group now. Money's no use now, Eggy. Money's cheap. Leverage, Eggy. Proper fucking leverage, that's what we need. You can't put a cash pric*the* on that. Time to do what it takes, Eggy, and throw the bitch in the blaze.'

Letting those cryptic, chilling words hang there, Terrence finally takes my hand. I haul him to his feet. He takes a moment, breathing deeply at the burst of effort. Closer now, less shadow up here than down there, I notice the sallow complexion of his skin, the cold clammy grip of his hands as I help him up, the sunken sockets.

'Ex*th*cellent,' he rasps, labouredly. 'Onwards and upwards, hey.'

Then, with a twisting agony, he locks up from head to toe, his hand clutching at his chest, before pitching forward and crashing to the ground, stiff as a board, his head thwacking painfully against the cobbles.

11

Tear was right, you know. It's not a game I can afford to play. Still, silver linings are reaped where you sow them. Wait, is that right?

I had rather thought it a good idea, you know. Heading to London with Tear. If I'm being honest with you, I didn't have the guts to go on my own. I found I couldn't leave the bath in Bath. I wanted to. I wanted to come straight to London, but I couldn't. What if no one remembered me? Worse still, what if they absolutely remembered me, remembered everything? It felt a lot better travelling with someone. And that that someone should be Terrence bloody Chalambert. Hurrah. I could surf in on the back of his coattails. Stand next to him while he was newly minted and bask in some reflected glory. Let the people know that Eggy was back and what a fine Eggy of a man he was – sunny side up and perfectly normal.

The right corner of my lip draws up in a sneer. I'm not… sneering. Although, I could. God, I'm contemptible.

In the cold, sobering light of defeat I realise I should have scarpered off at the Bridewaters', left Terrence behind to his strange bloody family and their frightful ways. But honestly, when you murder a horse, you get completely lost in the insanity of it all.

Can't say Tear Bear would agree, but I for one am quite glad he had a heart attack. Gave me time to think, to see things straight.

My sneer disappears. My lip drops back to its resting position as the nurse finishes stitching up my cheek.

It's not a game I can afford to play, but equally, now that I'm in it, it's not one I can afford to walk away from. Not with Terrence anyhow. Should the Bridewaters and the papers drag me into their one-sided allegations, I might be able to survive it. Thrive, possibly. After all, there's nothing wrong with a *minor* scandal. Only those of a certain social stature are allowed a scandal. I think I'd qualify, being a hero and all. It displays the kind of uncaring, straight-speaking, rugged individualism that society so highly lauds these days. But there's a fine line between cheeky scandal and public disgrace. And the line demarcating those two eventualities, mark my words, is tracked out by a pair of nuns and a black-and-blue bleeding grandma! Bloody Nora!

No. I'd be ruined. The bank would cast me out for proper this time, barred from the City completely. Hell, word would be so great I'd probably be lucky even to keep a job in somewhere as backwards as Montreal.

If I'm being honest with you, the bank didn't ask me to leave London; they told me to. It's America or the bin. They'd have fired me right off the bat, of course, but I'm a war hero, don't you know. America was the humane thing to do.

I've been good across the pond. I was good in New York and I'm good in Montreal. Perfectly proper. That's why I take such long lunches now. I get all my crying done at lunch.

If I'm being honest with you, that's what the bank didn't like. Nobody likes it. A grown man crying at his desk.

Everything turns white and pain explodes across my face. FUCK ME. That's the doctor resetting my nose. I'm informed it was horribly crooked. I'm crying again, but that's because of the nose. It's more that my eyes are watering, not really crying. Not that the doctor minds, anyway. You get a free pass with a doctor. Or at least to your face you do. I'm sure they laugh about it at lunch. The doctor decided I'd had enough medication for the time being. That's why the nose hurt: nothing to take the edge off. I told him I hadn't had any medication, no anaesthetic whatsoever. He chuckled at that.

I look down jealously at Tear. He's got two beds, the fat bastard. Two beds all to himself. All I've got is this hard, bony chair.

All I wanted to do was come back to London, you know. Get back in the good books of the Old Boys Club. I don't like Canada. I like London. And now, I've just got here and I have to leave. Isn't that cruel? But I can't go visit those wiry moustaches in the City now, can I? Look at me, I look like a battered cabbage. They'd think me decidedly odd turning up like this, like I've gone off the deep end… again.

Best I head back to Canada, I suppose. Try again… try again in a year or two, I suppose. What's another year or two, hey? Give me time to re-repress those old memories. Bottle them up nice and tight and hide them somewhere nice and dark. Goodbye Passchendaele, off you shuffle now.

The doctor's done and gone. But it's not long before Terrence and I have some more company. The tall, angular chap that tried to capture Tear at the station strides in. You know, the one with the knock-off suit, the shoddy brogues, the stubble, the cheap cologne – you know. Poor imitations aside, the bastard moves like a viper. Cold reptilian eyes to boot.

Don't worry, I'm expecting him. I don't just get to walk away from all this, do I? I'm in a tricky spot. Too risky to continue forwards, too risky to stop. That's why I've spoken with Tear's sister, Tabitha. Vengeful fury and implacable willpower to one side, she seems very nice. Lovely telephone voice. I've cut a deal. She can have Terrence in return for making sure she hushes up all this potential scandal and disgrace. She's as keen to ensure the family name isn't dragged into all this as much as I am mine.

''ello, 'ello,' says the viper with a smile. His face is in a bad way, but not as bad as his hands apparently. Blood seeps through the thick gauze wrapped around them. 'Pleasure to meet you again, Mr Whistle. We weren't formally introduced last time. My names 'Arry and I'll be taking care of proceedings.'

'Don't hurt me!' I blurt out, suddenly not quite so sure of myself.

Harry laughs. 'You can relax, Mr Whistle. No hard feelings. Just business, at the end of the day.' He looks at Terrence. 'Well, no mistaking this one, is there?' He reaches into his jacket pocket. I tense just in case. 'Here you are, Mr Whistle.'

I relax. It's an envelope. I asked Tabitha for a spot of money, explained to her the situation. I take it. It's a fat one. That's nice. Pocketing it, I stand up and push off.

Don't worry though, I've left a note behind. *Gone back to Canada. Eggy.*

12

I stop at the top of the hospital steps and take in the view. For the first time since arriving, I really just stop and breathe it in. *London.* Gosh. There's no place like it, you know, there really isn't. I watch the people as they shuffle on by. Everybody caught up in their own little world. Everyone ever so slightly miserable but content in the fact that everyone else is just as modestly miserable as they. There's no place like it. It's the collective apathy, it envelopes you in a warm embrace and says, 'Don't worry. It's not your problem. It's not *your* problem.' It's a powerful freedom. I take a moment more, assuring myself, promising myself that I'll be back. Goodbye for *now* old girl, but not goodbye.

I proceed gingerly down the steps. Lordy, I'm sore. I cross the street, heading for the District line. If I get a move on, I can catch a train from Victoria to Portsmouth and be on a ferry back bright and early tomorrow morning. I could stay a night in the big smoke but, unlikely or not, I'm rather worried about bumping into some-one; about actually meeting someone, looking how I do. I think I'd rather peel off. Play it safe.

I'm heading down the steps of South Kensington station when something catches my eye. Turning, I close my blurry left eye to remove the confusion and suck it all up with my right. *Good Lord. GOOD LORD!*

An icy punch lodges in the pit of my stomach. I stagger forward. I grab a newspaper from the stand. *Good. Lord.* My legs give way and I crumple. Right in front of the stand, I crumple. I stay there. Despairing. Completely and utterly despairing. No room for anything else.

On the ground in front of me, on the front page of the news-paper on the ground in front of me fluttering in the breeze, along-side Tear, is *me*. There's my face on the front page. The front of my face is on the very front of the front page of the newspaper.

I want to be sick. I want to cry. But there's no room for any of that.

I try to read but the words won't stick. The narrative won't hold, but it doesn't matter. The few words I latch onto are clear enough. EGBERT WHISTLE. ACCOMPLICE. WANTED. BRIDEWATERS. NUNS. THREATS. INTIMIDATION. ROBBERY. ASSAULT. It's all there in black and white. Ruin.

Empty, I lie crumpled on the paving while my world, my hopes and dreams, crumble around me to the sound of "Ere, mate. You gonna pay for that?' and "Ere mate. Do you mind, you're scaring off my customers,' and "Ere, mate. Are you alright?'

And then I begin to feel something. I *really* begin to feel something.

* * *

I stop, hunched over on the pavement, dry heaving. Trying to heave out all the sickness – but my stomach's empty from all the other times. *I feel sick.*

I need to get to the hospital. I need to get off the street. I need to get back to the hospital. People are staring at me. Some are carrying newspapers. I stumble back from them fearfully, I stumble to the ground, I stumble back on all fours, strands of mucous lace across my gaping mouth. I wipe them away, attempting to look respectable, attempting to look normal, to look fine, just fine.

I'm breathing but it's not working. I breathe faster, but that works even less. I have less air. It doesn't matter. I need to get to the hospital. I need to get to Tear. Before he wakes up. Before he knows. He can fix this, can't he? He can sort all this out. I *need* Tear to fix this. I need Tear.

I'm back on my feet, running. Horns blare as I race blindly across the road.

He did warn me, didn't he? Tear did warn me. He did say she's a spiteful bitch. *She's a spiteful bitch.*

Anger surges inside me. I'm angry. I don't deserve this. Well, maybe I do. I don't know. But we had a deal. *We had an agreement.*

I sprint through the hospital. Across a ward and along a corridor, before bursting through the door of the private room housing my treasure.

'Harry, listen…'

Fuck. There's no Harry to plead my case with… and no Terrence to plead for. There's no Tear. Tear Bear. Shit. He's gone. Why's he gone? Where's he gone? FUCK, HE'S FUCKING GONE. I'M FUCKED.

My breathing's gone all funny again. I force myself to think. This can't be the end. This shan't be the end. The bed! The mattress. The mattress is still dented. I squash my face into the head-shaped impression. It's still warm and fetid. No, not fetid; floral. It smells floral. Confused, I lift my head. The mattress. THE MATTRESS. Singular, not plural. Tear Bear was on two beds, not one. I'm in the wrong room!

I fire out the door and collide with a startled nurse. 'Where is he? Where's Tear? Tear Bear. You know, the fat man? The enormous fat man, which room?' I demand, grabbing her by the shoulders.

The nurse doesn't answer, just stares back, startled. I take her by the shoulders and give her a good jostle. 'Where, damn you?

Quickly now.' She still doesn't answer, mouth all agape. I jostle her again. I give her a real good jostle. That's what you do, isn't it? When someone's stuck, you jostle them, by the shoulders. You jostle their thoughts loose. 'Please, where is he? Where?' I demand again with another jostle, but different this time from my previous jostles. I must not have been doing it right before. I'm giving her small but very fast jostles now. She's vibrating. I'm vibrating her.

'He's, he's there. He's just there,' quivers the nurse, nodding to a door further down the corridor. Success. 'Fourth door down, door on the left.'

'Thank you!' I call as I dash away.

I burst into Tear's room! No, no, I don't. Fourth, fourth door on the left. Why can't I remember? My brain's not working.

I burst into Tear's room – third time's a charm. 'Harry, listen…' There's no Harry. Thank God! There is a Tear though. Thank you, God!

'Eggy?'

Shit. He's awake. He's looking at me. Shit. What does he know? Shit. Why's he awake? He's meant to be asleep. That stingy nob of a doctor! I told him to *double* the dose, *triple it*! Terrence chomps through that stuff like water.

'Eggy, what's going on? Where am I? What fucking time is it, Eggy? What's happened? What's happening?'

Oh, thank God for that. He's ignorant. *Thank you, God.*

'Why am I strapped to the fucking bed, Eggy? What the fuck is going on?'

My giddy aunts. What the hell is going on? Three leather straps encircle Tear and the bed – the beds! He struggles determinedly against the restraints but to no avail.

'Speak, Eggy. Fucking talk.' He's frothing at the mouth, the veins in his face fit to burst as he heaves and cramps.

'No, Tear. Stop! You need to take it *easy*. You've just had a heart attack. You've just had a bloody heart attack!'

Tear freezes. 'A heart attack. Good Lord! Am I, am I alright?'

'How the hell should I know?! Do you feel alright?'

'… No. Where am I?'

'Where do you think? The hospital.'

'Well why am I strapped to a bloody hos*th*pital bed?'

'You're, you're a violent sleeper. It was for your own…'

'What's that?'

'What's what?'

'That.' I follow the direction of Tear's nod. SHIT. The note. I think he's spotted the note. He's definitely spotted the note. You can't miss it! I placed it quite perfectly, leaning between the glass and the jug of water, perfectly easy to spot. That was the whole point! Fuck.

'Gone back to Canada. Eggy,' reads Tear, perplexed. '… Eggy, are you leaving?'

'What? No. No, I'm not leaving.' I brush the note off and pour myself a glass of water. Buying time. *Cooling down.* 'I'm not leaving you. I'm not leaving you,' I repeat, and it isn't a lie. 'It's just a… joke, that's all.' Which *is* a lie. A poor one. 'Just a… silly, silly old joke.'

Tear looks from the note to the leather straps tying him to the bed. Then he looks at me. I look at him and he looks at me. I attempt to take a nonchalant sip of water but my jittering hand spills it all over me.

When Tear finally speaks again he does so quietly, and I find the whole room has turned an icy, frigid cold. 'Eggy, what have you done? What have you done, Eggy?'

'Nothing. Nothing.' I try to look away, but Tear's venomous, jaundiced eyes won't let me.

'… Eggy?… Eggy?'

'I'm sorry, Tear,' I whisper. 'I'm really bloody sorry, Tear. It was a mistake. I can see that now. It was a stupid bloody mistake.'

'What was, Eggy? What?'

'I sold you out, Tear. I sold you out to your sister. She said she'd take care of me. Take care of everything – in return for you. Only she lied, Tear. *The fucking bitch lied!* I'm all over the papers. We're all over the papers! I'm ruined. I'm ruined.' Oh bollocks. I'm crying again. Not a panicked cry. Not a terrified cry. A very small, very sad cry. Those are the worst.

Tear keeps on looking at me, simply looking, strapped to the bed looking like a corpse. Quiet as a corpse.

'I'm sorry, Tear. I'm sorry. But you'd had a heart attack. A fucking *heart attack*. You weren't responsive. Don't be mad. Please don't be mad. I'm back. I'm here to help.' I'm getting worked up now. I bash the wall with my fists. An exhibition of my sorrow. I'm *sorry*.

Tear glances at the door, worriedly. 'Alwight, alwight, alwight, Eggy. It's alwight.'

'It's not alright is it, though? I've ruined everything!'

'Eggy. Eggy. Eggy. It's alwight. I'm not *mad*. I'm *not* mad. I'd… I'd've most cthertainly done the same in your shoes.'

'You… you would?' I stop my banging.

'Of coursthe. Logical. Logical. We can fix this, Eggy. But first I need you…'

'I'm ruined, Tear. I'm ruined.' I'm on the floor now, breathing funny.

'Eggy. *Eggy*. I need you to unstrap me. I need you to *unstrap me*.'

'I'm ruined, fucking ruined.' I'm not talking to Tear now. I'm really just gasping and making sounds.

'*Eggy*, I need you to…' Tear stops. He takes a deep breath. 'Don't be sthilly, Eggy. Ruined? This is all nothing more than a cheeky scandal. We'll make it all go away. Puff. Gone.'

'Gone?' I repeat.

'My family,' continues Tear, 'has a closthe welationship with the bank, you know. I can get you a job there if you like? If you want, it's yours, scandal or not.'

'You can?' I ask, my breath finally steadying.

'Would you like that, Eggy? Would you like to come back to England, Eggy? Work at the bank?'

'Which… which bank?'

'Which bank?' says Tear with a smile. It's a silly, child-friendly smile. It makes me feel nice. '*The* bank. The Bank of England, Eggy.' My eyes go wide with amazement. Perspiration beads down Tear's sick-looking face. 'But to do that, Eggy, we need to get out of here. You follow? I need you to stay calm and focus*th*ed. We need to leave before they get here. Do you understand?'

'Oh, no. They're already here, Tear,' I inform him with my own little child-friendly smile. 'Harry, the man from the station, he's already here. He came, so I left. Then I came back. I'm back, Tear.'

Tear's yellow complexion hollows out to a deathly white.

'Well, where is he, Eggy?' he rasps.

'I don't know, popped out for a cuppa?'

'Eggy… get me out of these *fucking* straps. *Get me out the fucking straps right fucking now, Eggy. Eggy. Eggy.*'

He hasn't finished Eggying me but I'm already on my feet, at the straps. The situation has, I think, finally, fully caught up with me. I'm all, *ALL*, over the straps but they just won't go! I'm all thumbs, ten bloody drunken thumbs. Oh Christ.

'Quicker, Eggy. Do it quicker,' urges Tear, his voice cracking with the pressure.

I fail on the third buckle just as I have with the rest. I go back to trying my luck with the first.

'For Christ's s*th*ake. Stop. Stop. Just stop a moment,' snaps Tear. I stop. Useless and ashamed.

'Eggy, look at me. Look up.' I look. 'You're in this until you're out. Do you hear me? Until you're out, you're in. S*th*o pull yourself together, man. Because you're… Oh, cock.'

'Mr Whistle. Ah, and Mr Chalambert, good to see you're awake, sir. Looking well.' Oh bollocks. It's Harry, smiling in the doorway, cuppa in hand. 'What can I do you for, Mr Whistle?'

'Oh, hello. Just came back for…' – I cast around, nonchalantly, for something, *anything!* – '…for a spot of water. Jolly hot out there, hey?' I pick up the glass jug and pour into the already-full glass.

The water spills over the top and across the small table. I don't stop. I carry on pouring with my tremoring hand.

Harry doesn't say anything. Doesn't comment. Instead, he steps confidently forward from the doorway, turning slightly to his left as he pushes the door closed behind him. That's lucky. His right eye is the swollen one, so he doesn't see it coming when I shatter the jug into the side of his head with my left hand.

There's a moment, a brief beat, where Harry just stays there, swaying woozily on the spot. Then he crumples.

I remain where I am, breathing heavily. It wasn't much exertion, glassing him, but I'm breathing heavily nonetheless.

'Good, Eggy. Good. Now get me out these straps. Quickly now.'

I'm back at the straps, attacking the buckles with all my thumbs.

Then I'm being pulled off of the buckles, away from the bed. It's Harry, back on his feet. He's grabbed me from behind, wrapped me up in a bear hug as he wrestles me back. He would have been better off just jabbing me with a piece of broken glass, or, failing that, clobbering me with a fist, a fist straight to the back of my skull, but – like me – I don't think he's thinking straight. He tightens his arms around me. Silently, furiously constricting me. I glance behind and find his mangled, bleeding head is inches from my own. A flap of skin with a shard of glass still hanging from it drapes down loosely over that blackened, swollen right eye of his. It's a ghastly picture. Terrifying. Made all the more so by his lack of sound. He makes no sound, just constricts me with inhuman strength.

I don't know what to do. I don't know how to combat this. My head feels fit to burst. I think my stitches have burst open.

As Harry squeezes, he drags me back. Without anything else to do, with barely a thought not yet squeezed and pushed from my head, I cling on to Terrence. Terrence is the key. Terrence is the answer. That's all I can think. *Hold on to Tear. Hold on to Tear.*

My feet are off the ground now, my arms stretched thin. All of my energy, all of my focus and strength in my hands: d*on't let go.* Then everything starts to go hazy. Everything starts to go funny. Like my funny breathing from before, except, I realise, this time I'm simply not breathing at all.

My grip begins to give. I'm stretched further backwards, my grip stretched further out. I'm right on the brink! And then so is the bed – the beds! They're right on the brink. From my strung-out, soft-focused mind I clock that the beds are tipping. *They're tipping over.*

Everything blurs as the beds pass the point of no return and slam down onto their side, Tear crashing to the ground with them. My grip rips loose in the commotion and Harry and I thud into the wall behind, punching halfway through the plaster. Harry takes the worst of it, sandwiched between me and the wall.

But still the bastard doesn't let go! HE WON'T LET GO! I struggle impotently while watching Tear struggle too. He's still strapped to the beds. The buckles haven't given an inch, but he's managed to jostle onto his front, the beds now bearing down straight on top of him. With a great heave, he pushes to his knees, and then to his feet. The beds, still strapped to his back, tower above him and then behind him as he straightens up. He totters forward a few steps, securing his balance. I cry for him to help me, but he pays me no notice whatsoever, stumbling instead for the door. He throws it wide and rushes at the opening. He doesn't get far. The beds catch in the door frame. They're too big. Too big by half to fit. Terrence backs up and tries again, angling and ducking and heaving. He's an enormous hellish puzzle piece. No thought at all, just mad determination, determined to fit through any which way.

At the same time, I, exercising my last few drops of energy, struggle with Harry in much the same manner as Tear does with the door, desperate to free myself.

Except Tear's done it. He's on the other side. One moment he's with me, the next he's not. It seems like some bizarre optical illusion, some strange trick of the light, but somehow Tear's on the other side of the door and I'm not. I'm not. I'm not with Tear. I'm here on the floor with Harry, a man possessed, having the very thread of life squeezed out from me.

'Tear! Tear!' I rasp from my tortured, empty lungs, but Tear continues to pay me no notice. Penguin-like, he waddles down the corridor as fast as his still bed-bound legs will let him. A doctor moves to stop him but thinks better of it and ducks to one side as Tear goes past, a swinging bed leg taking the shocked doctor out just as he thought it was safe to stand back up.

Then he's gone. Tear's gone from sight. Completely. My Tear Bear has gone and I'm alone. *I'm alone. I've lost my Tear Bear!*

… But I'm not alone am I? I'm with Harry. I'm in here and not out there because of Harry. My life is about to be ruined. Over. Completely and utterly over, forever, because of Harry. I feel a great anger surge inside me. *A GREAT ANGER.* I felt it before, after seeing the papers, but I smothered it. It's not good to feel anger. You wouldn't like me when I'm angry. That's what people say, isn't it? You wouldn't like me when I'm angry. It's a silly thing to say because no one likes anyone when they're angry. *We don't like angry people.* That being said though: you wouldn't like me when I'm angry. And I'm angry now. I'm fucking *raging.* This is all fucking wrong. *It's all fucking wrong.*

I'm whipping my head back, repeatedly. It smashes against Harry's nose, against Harry's face, repeatedly. I repeat my repetitions until his grip finally begins to give. I'm facing him now. My face is facing his face now. The large flap of skin above his eye slaps against my cheek and eyes as I throttle him, shake him. As I snarl and hate him and hurt him.

I'm not with Harry now. I'm standing. Harry's still on the floor. He doesn't look too good. A doctor has me, he's pulled me off. I'm snarling at him now. He's not holding me now. Not after I looked at him.

I'm racing out the door now. I'm searching for Terrence now.

Nobody knows where he went. How can they not know where

he went? He was wearing hospital beds, WEARING HOSPITAL BEDS!

I'm on the street demanding to know which way he went. I'm jostling people, I'm really fucking *jostling* them, but it's not working this time. FUCK. It's not working. *FUCK.* Where's Terrence? *Where's my Tear Bear?*

13

A couple pass by mere feet from me, apparently enjoying the clammy night air, the thick, dark heat that refuses to lift. The lady's tinkling laughter mocks me as they go. I dare them, I just dare them to look down, to see me, to meet me in the eyeballs. Not so pleasant a night now, is it? Go on, meet me in all my eyeballs. I'm cocooned in my beady little balls. Festooned in my own face. Take a good long look, you rich, privileged fucks.

A thorn pricks me as I soften at their departure. It pricks that damn thought loose. *I've lost my Tear Bear.* I'm fucked. I'm doomed. *Doomed.* It's not a bed of roses I find myself in is it? Except it is – I'm lying in a bed of roses in Regents Park, wrapped in reams of the evening paper. I spent every penny, every penny, buying every paper I could, every paper I could carry. God, I was angry. I'm still angry now, but I was more angry then. I've settled down to a simmer now. I'm all over the papers. I'm on every paper that's on me – and there's a lot of paper on me. I'm camouflaged in myself. It's wretched.

I've lost my Tear Bear. It would be nice to think that he hasn't forgotten me. Or rather he's forgotten just enough but not too much. It'd be nice to think he's forgotten about the whole betrayal but not forgotten what jolly company I am; that really, I'm a good, honest, innocent chap. But I can't think that – because I don't believe it.

At this point though, what do Terrence's feelings toward me really matter? After all, we're both damned. There's not a snowball's hope in hell of him making it to the signing tomorrow. I'd be amazed if he even survives the night – literally, not figuratively. Tear is penniless, morbidly obese and recovering from a heart attack after being beaten bloody by a mob; hunted for by his sister and her private hounds, as well as by most of his family and friends; wanted by the police for robbery and assault, with his name and picture all over the evening papers (as are mine); oh, and did I not mention, he was last seen, rather conspicuously I have to say, with two bloody hospital beds strapped to his back.

I don't think it pessimistic at this point to say that Tear is doomed. And if he's doomed, I'm doomed too. *I've lost my Tear Bear.* I'm not leaving though; I'm not running away. My spite is all built up now. I'm not going anywhere, I'm too full of spite. I'm heavy with it. I'm not running, fuck 'em. I want to see how this all pans out. I want to see what happens. Then I'll run. You can bet your life on it. Then I'll run. Catch me if you can, you rotten fucking scoundrels.

It's all very bad for me. Getting like this, getting like that. Getting like I was at the hospital. I don't care. Fuck 'em. *Fuck 'em.* Fuck that Harry. Best place he could be, a hospital. It's very bad for me, you know. I was really angry, you know. I'm still angry now, but I was more angry then. Then, I was raging. Absolutely raging. Utterly, shakingly, quakingly raging. It's very bad for me. Feeling like that. The last time I felt like that, the last time I had the shaky quakes, I had to leave for America. That's how bad it is. I had been crying at my desk, which was a poor choice of location – but if I didn't cry at my desk, I feared I'd smash it to pieces. Mr Jenkins told me to pull myself together, to stop being so pathetic. I stopped crying but that had the regrettable and immediate effect of inducing the shaky quakes. I bit off one of Mr Jenkins' mutton chops. I felt terribly guilty. He was a nice chap, Mr Jenkins. Thank goodness I'm a war hero – in most circumstances gnawing off a superior's left-side sideburn would be grounds for instant dismissal.

A war hero. Look at me now: lying in my bed of roses, wrapped in front-page photos of me with my medal. I'm not really a hero. I just have a medal. A Victoria Cross. If Victoria knew the truth, she would be cross.

They took two photos of me in the war. One was after Passchendaele. The other was in a fancy room in London with my medal. In Passchendaele, I'm in a trench. I was never in a trench, but in the photo I am. I had to clear out some sepoys spoiling the background, but it turned out well – I look very rugged, like a soldier. There was a reporter with the photographer. He asked me how we were doing in the war. I said something along the lines of 'Fuck, bugger, cock, bollocks, and cunt.' I was still quite wired. But all they reported was 'Egbert Whistle says, "Keep up the good fight, troops".' So much censorship. God forbid we show the truth, give an honest view.

They've used the 'fancy room' photo in the paper, the cleaner one. The one of me in a clean room with a clean shave. It's a stronger juxtaposition I suppose.

That was the first time I ever got the shaky quakes – the time I earned my medal, Passchendaele. I shot a man, you know. Shot two men in fact, shot them dead. And neither man was the man I was trying to shoot. That's where the shaky quakes get you. Killing all the wrong people. I shot two Germans, poor chaps.

I scrunch a handful of papers into a nice thick, head-sized ball. I then take an uncreased front page from a stack next to me and carefully wrap my black and white face around the ball of scrunched papers. I stare at me. Me stares back. Fuck him. Fuck that me. I lie there, waiting for me to go to sleep. Don't turn your fucking back on him. Don't even blink.

14

Tuesday, June 19th 1923

My parents had the good grace to die when I was seven. They sold fish at a market. They earned just enough not to know how poor they were. As a result of their unexpected cremation, my sister and I were deposited in the care of an uncle who had stolen his riches in India. We were a sad reminder of the life he had spent a good deal of money buying himself out of. He sent us away to boarding school. I went to a good one – not a great one, but good enough that it could beat the poverty out of me and the breeding into me. Naturally, my uncle died penniless and scorned. I wonder what they'd think, my parents, if they could see me?

My spite has all leaked out now. Now I simply feel sad. Quite sad. I've not ducked out though. I'm here, loitering on a bench in Lincoln's Inn Fields. I shuffled out from my den in Regents Park first thing and hobbled across, taking in the sights as I went. Gosh, I've missed this place. In the distance, across the road and slightly to my left, is the door. Number 16. I'm hiding behind yesterday's paper. It's a bold move – but so far so good.

It all seems very normal. Everything seems *extremely* normal. I expected there to be suspicious sets of eyes pointing in all directions; hard men doing their best to look casual; police officers trying to go unnoticed – but there aren't.

Someone who I assume was Tabitha has already headed inside. It looked like Tabitha, I think. I've only seen a picture of her before now. She was very small, Tabitha. She was in the distance, of course, so she would be – but even accounting for the yards she was small, like a little bird crossing the cobbles. What was most unsettling is that she was completely alone. Just Tabitha. I've seen no one else cross the threshold.

'Good for you, Eggy. I hoped you'd come.'

FUCKING HELL! I almost leap out of my skin. I spin to my left. *TERRENCE* sits next to me on the bench. Good Lord! He's alive. *He's only bloody alive.* Living and breathing! Right next to me! I'm SAVED! Terrence is here to save me. *Where the hell did he come from?!* Lord be praised! Tear Bear! Good Lord! *But seriously, how'd he sneak up on me? I'm supposed to be alert!*

'Tear!' I cry. And then I stop. I stop when I look at him. When I look at him, I stop. *Good Lord* indeed. He might be alive but he doesn't look well. He really doesn't look well. 'You're alive?' I ask, suddenly doubtful. The usual yellow-tinged, sallow complexion of his skin has been washed off and re-stained with a deathly grey, and his breathing comes in ragged little bursts. 'You… survived then?' I follow up.

'Thrived. I thrived, Eggy. After I left you, I threw myself, beds and all, into the Thames*th*. Paddled on my back across to the south bank. Spent the night laying low under a b*w*idge with some homeless folk. Good people, Eggy. Generous. Rich in spirit, those b*w*idge people. Helped me with my bed problem. Lis*th*ten. I hoped you'd come. I need you. You're a good f*w*iend, Eggy. I need a good f*w*iend.'

'R-really, you're not, you're not mad at me?'

'Cours*th*e not. Cours*th*e not, old bean. Before, everything before, that's… well, it's all beds under the b*w*idge.'

Lordy, this is all good news – great news! Terrence is here, and I'm his friend. I'm his *friend*… And yet I don't feel good. In spite of the good turn of events, I don't feel good. It's Tear. I felt a burst of goodness initially, but the longer I look at Tear the quicker that burst of relief recedes, the less good I feel. It's being swapped out with creeping concern. He *really* doesn't seem well: he's having trouble breathing, but appears oblivious to the difficulty; he scrubs absentmindedly but persistently at the spot where his heart should be and his wide eyes jitter back and forth as he talks; he's covered in grime and his clothes are now so torn that there's more sagging, bruised, scabbed and bloodied flesh on display than not. He looks worse than I do, and I look feral – the cut on my cheek seems to have become infected, a yellow pus oozing out in a steady stream. 'It's quiet, isn't it? Nic*th*e and quiet. Do you know why, Eggy? Do you know why there aren't threats posted on every corner?'

'No.'

'Leverage, Eggy. Leverage.' A sick grin blossoms on his sickly face.

'… I don't know what that means, Terrence.'

'I was up real early, just before dawn. Left the b*w*idge people behind and broke into a chemis*th*t. Got some supplies for my ex*th*pedition, for my fishing ex*th*pedition. Armed with supplies, I went fishing for leverage. Do you know where one fishes for leverage, Eggy?' Terrence pulls out a medicinal-looking bottle from one of his pockets and takes a good long draught.

'What's that, Tear?' I ask, nodding at the vial.

'Be damned if I know. That chemis*th*t I *w*obbed was all in Latin. Not classical Latin, not useful Latin, science Latin. So I took one of everything. Lis*th*ten, one goes fishing wherever the fish are.' Putting the bottle back, he picks up a large sack next to him – where the hell did that come from?! I'm not doing very well here. *I need to be more observant.* 'That's my leverage,' he says, nodding to the sack. 'In there's my leverage. Don't *look*. Do something for me, for your s*th*ake, and don't *look*. I need you to look after it. If you weren't here – it's good that you're here, Eggy, very good – if you weren't here, I'd have to leave my leverage under a bench or in a bush and should anything happen to my leverage, should they find my leverage, I fear I wouldn't be allowed to continue. They would stop me, Eggy. They would rescind my right of safe passage. Do you follow?'

I do not follow.

'I need you to look after the leverage, Eggy. Don't look. Lis*th*en. You stay here with the leverage and I'll potter across to the s*th*olic*th*itors*th*. When I call out – I'll call out from a window – when I call, you bring it up. That's when I'm safe. You unders*th*tand? When I call, it's done, you can bring it up. Can you do that for me, Eggy? Can you?' Tear's taken me by the collar and pulled me close to him. I can feel his warm breath on my open wound.

'I… I… can do that, Tear. No problem at all.'

'*Do what?*'

'Erm, erm… stay here with the bag, with the leverage. Then when you call, bring it across.'

'Good man, Eggy. We're going to be al*w*ight, you and I.' Tear gathers the top of the fabric sack and presses it into my hand, wrapping the drawstring around my fist. He really doesn't look well. 'Wait for my call, Eggy. Good man.' He pats my cheek. His thumb lands in my wound – it really hurts. 'Good Eggy.' He squeezes his thumb further into my bleeding cheek. 'Do you want to see, Eggy? Would you like to look?'

'… No.'

'Best you look, Eggy. Just in case you get spooked. You're easily spooked, Eggy.' Terrence takes the sack back. Heaving it into his lap, he pulls the top down.

* * *

It's a *child*. Terrence's leverage is a *child*. Tear's right, I shouldn't have looked! Why did he make me look? I didn't need to look!

Inside the sack on Terrence's lap is a bundle of linen. On top of the linen, in the foetal position, is a child. His leverage is a *child*. Whose child is this?! Where did he get a child from?! In the sack of leverage is a *child*. Not a fish, a *child*. It's a child!

'It's Gwendolyn,' rasps Terrence, proudly, looking around carefully before taking… Gwendolyn… by the head and pulling her up, halfway out the bag.

Good Lord. Gwendolyn doesn't look well either. And I say this as someone using Terrence as a reference point. Her little lips are a light shade of blue and her cheeks look waxy and cold.

'Gwendolyn here means the world to Tabitha.' Terrence lets go of Gwendolyn's head, taking her by the shoulders instead and bouncing her gently up and down on his knee as he speaks. Her head flip-flops back and forth as he does. 'She's barren, you see, Tabitha. Gwendolyn is the best she has. She's Tabitha's god-daughter, our niece twice removed, or something like that. Jewel of the family. I s*th*tole her this morning. Pinched her from her bed, then reached out to Tabitha and explained the situation. Explained what I needed, what Gwendolyn needed really, for her s*th*afety… and mine.'

'What… what's wrong with her, Tear?'

'What?' responds Tear, oblivious, turning Gwendolyn so he can look. 'She's jus*th*t sleeping, Eggy. A good sleep. I gave her something to help her sleep. Keep her quiet, manageable.'

'What did you give her?' I ask, timidly.

'How the hell should I know, Eggy? It was all in Latin – haven't you been lis*th*tening?'

'She's not well, Tear. I think she needs help. We need to get her help.'

'Don't be bloody s*th*tupid. We can't get her help. She's the leverage, Eggy. She's the fucking leverage,' snaps Tear, using one hand to rummage through the pockets of his soiled overalls. 'I'll just wake her up, alright? I'll get her going. But if she screams, if she starts whining, it's on you, Eggy. She's all yours.'

He brings out a medicine bottle and, using his teeth, pries the lid off, spitting it to one side before sniffing the contents. 'Fuck.'

The bottle joins the lid on the ground as Terrence returns with growing agitation to his pocket search. His hand emerges again. 'Hah-hah!' He sniffs success this time. He presses the bottle between Gwendolyn's lips, tipping her head back and pouring liberally. 'There we go. There we are. D*w*ink up. D*w*ink up.' Except she's not drinking. The viscous brown liquid dribbles out of her full mouth and closed throat, running down her neck and little shoulders before eventually dropping from her fingertips and pooling about her feet. '*Fuck. Fuck.*' Abandoning the bottle feed, Terrence turns his fraying temper upon me. 'Lis*th*ten, lis*th*ten, just look after her, Eggy,' he says, shoving her frantically back in the sack. 'You look after her. We'll deal with this later. We'll fix this after.' Tear pulls the drawstring tight around a folded, shunted Gwendolyn. The sack is forced upon me. Tear gestures towards number 16: 'Over there is everything. This, this is nothing. It's fine. It's alright, Eggy. It's all alright.' Before he's even finished speaking he's already on his feet, walking quickly away.

'No, Tear,' I call after him, summoning my courage. 'You can't bloody well leave her with me. She's in a state. She needs help. I can't stay with her. What if I should be found out? What then? What about me, hey? I can't, Tear. I can't stay with her. I won't.'

Terrence pauses mid-step. He turns slowly back to me, and I find myself fixed, trapped even, in the furious, mocking contempt that washes off him in waves. He's back, up real close to me now. My nostrils are full of him, full of that sharp, acrid sweat. I try not to breathe it in but it's rather tricky. I'm rather scared. I'm scared. Why am I scared? It's Tear Bear, I reassure myself. But every time I lean into the comforting knowledge that it's my Tear Bear, I find my reassurance dissolves under that pungent odour, bleached of utility by the scathing look radiating from those bloodshot eyes.

'What did you s*th*ay… Eggy?'

'I… I… said, sorry, old bean, but I can't, simply can't, you understand, stay here with, with… Gwendolyn. I could take her somewhere though. How about that? Get her, get her feeling top notch. It's no problem. No problem at all.'

'No, Eggy. You're going to stay here with her. *Wight* here. Do you know why?'

'Em… em… because that's, that's the plan, your, your plan.'

Terrence leans in even closer. My view, my little world, darkens as daylight is eclipsed by his massive frame, as I find myself caught in the centre of his expanding shadow.

'You're going to stay here becaus*the* I told you to, Eggy,' he says softly, scathingly. 'That's why. Becaus*the* you're mine, Eggy. Becaus*the* I own you. You're not going anywhere becaus*the* I *own* you, Eggy. I'm fully confident you shall do as you're told – becaus*the* you're mine. Becaus*the* if you don't, I shall dash you on the rocks. Becaus*the* if you don't, I shan't help you. I'll never fix any of this… Look around, will you?' He's whispering now: 'My s*thisth*ter had everything at her disposal: time, money, people, influence, power. All I had… was you: a pathetic, spent, washed-up soldier. And yet here I am, walking to my birthright unmoles*thth*ted. Why? Becaus*the* I own you, Eggy. I own what I need, and my s*thisth*ter can't buy that. Do you know why my legs didn't work, Eggy, before? Becaus*the* I didn't want them to. I wanted to guilt you to my side. I wanted to leverage your naive disposition. But you couldn't even get that *wight*, could you. Couldn't even get me on a t*w*ain. So, I b*w*ought my legs back. Then I saw the paper, the story in the paper, knew flakey Eggy was likely to bolt when the potential consequences dawned on him. So what did I do? I *w*obbed a pair of nuns, *wight* in front of you, to implicate you. Then, at Ex*the*ter, while you went to get the tickets, I went off and sent a telegram, shopped you into the papers*th*, told them where to get a nic*the* picture of you. And in doing so I bound you to me. Even when I was unconscious and you t*w*ied to run, to betray me, you couldn't becaus*the* I'd made you mine. You're mine, Eggy. Mine to ruin and mine to save. So be a good chap and look after Gwendolyn.' With a last nerve-snapping look of hateful villainy he turns back around, done with me. He takes a step forward, then stops. 'You know, Eggy,' he says, looking forward, looking away, 'if I were Tabitha, and Gwendolyn had been taken, I wouldn't have yielded. I would have said "Smash the silly little thing to pieces, for all I care." That's why that foolish woman can't be me – she doesn't have what it takes. It wouldn't be a week before she was begging for a safe space where the mean men couldn't get her. That's why I'm here, Eggy.'

15

Terrence has left. Pottered off to his big date. I'm still here – on a bench with Gwendolyn, just like he told me to be. He said some rather awful things, Terrence. He's done some rather awful things… to me. But that's alright. Those awful things are out there, and right now I'm in here.

I'm in the bag. My head's in the bag with Gwendolyn. It's not so roomy in here, but I needed to get in. I need to get *real close*. Have a real thorough inspection. 'Hello, Gwendolyn,' I whisper. She doesn't respond. One of my hands and its corresponding arm have joined my head in the bag. I wipe off the medicinal residue staining her chin. My hand continues on. It's searching for a pulse. I'm feeling for a heartbeat. I'm deep in the sack, rummaging around for a heartbeat. THERE! *There!* Shit. I've lost it. Was it real? I'm rummaging once more. THERE! I've got it this time. I've got it! A pulse. There's a pulse. THANK THE LORD! There's a pulse. Wait! Shit, no. That's my thigh. I can feel the fear pulsing through my thigh through the fabric of the sack. *FUCK!* I'm searching again, pyretic in my search. My second arm joins the first – I have engaged all my arms! *FUCK!* Where's the beat? Where's her fucking heartbeat? I have an ear pressed firmly to her little chest. I'm listening, searching, looking out for any kind of beat. There's no beat. *Oh no.* It's true. It's true. She has no beat. Gwendolyn, the little girl in the sack, she's lost her beat! She's fucking beatless. I have a beatless little Gwendolyn in a sack.

… Now there's a beat. In the sack, there's a proper fucking beat now. Don't fool yourself, it's not Gwendolyn's. It's mine. It's my beat. My head's throbbing. My heart's thumping, beating me up from the inside out. My whole sack-surrounded world is beating and shaking. That *monstrosity*. Everything he said, everything he's done, that's in the sack too, now. *That cruel bastard.* He's ruined me. He's implicated me; sold me; smeared me; shredded my *future*; pissed his brown, liver-ruptured noxious urine all over my hopes and desires. He's ruined my reputation. Dressed me up as a fucking criminal. He's ruined me. *He's the one that fucking ruined me.*

'Excuse me, sir? Is everything alright?'

I freeze. I stop. My raging heart slams to a standstill as my mind constricts. There was a voice, you heard it. But perhaps it wasn't for me. I stay hiding in the sack, don't bother to venture out. Best I stay here, I reckon. Perhaps the voice wasn't aimed at me; if I come out now, then they'll notice me. I don't want to be noticed. I can't be noticed. *Gwendolyn.* I can't be noticed with Gwendolyn. I'm looking right at her. Trapped in the sack with her. My eyelashes brush her nose when I blink.

I feel faint.

'Sir?' comes the voice again.

I remain as I am.

A hand touches my shoulder. 'Sir?' *Shit.*

Timidly, reluctantly, I emerge back into the daylight. The blood drains from my face. I scrunch the top of the sack closed, quick as I can, and clutch it fearfully. It's a *policeman. A policeman.*

As I emerge, the officer jerks back with revulsion at the sight of my mangled noodle. *Shit.* He's not meant to be here. There's not meant to be anyone like him here. That's what the leverage is for! *He shouldn't be here. I have a dead girl in a sack.*

'What were you doing in there? What's in the sack?' demands

the officer, his polite tone turning cold with disgust at the appalling state of me.

'In here? N-nothing. My, my belongings. Just my life, simple as it is,' I answer, head bowed, staring at the ground. Desperately trying to appear pitiful, completely useless – it's hardly a stretch.

The officer leans down to my level, folding at the waist, back still straight as a rod. *Gosh, he's got some core strength, hasn't he?* I think briefly before returning to more pressing matters. He reaches out and takes a firm hold of the top of the sack. *Fuck.*

'Give it…' he stops mid-sentence. His gaze has been caught by something on the bench to my left. My eyes flick across. *Double fuck.* The paper. My face staring out from the front page. The officer looks from the paper to me. He's clocked it. That's the look of a man who has clocked it. How, I don't even know. In my current state I barely look like a *person*, any kind of person, let alone the well-dressed, clean-shaven, respectable young man in the photo. Bloody Nora, who is this officer? Sherlock Holmes? That's just my bloody luck.

I give the officer what I hope is a winning smile and say, 'Could be my long-lost brother, hey?'

The officer doesn't respond. His hand drifts to the truncheon secured at his hip and I buckle under the weight of my terror. I surge to my feet and run. It's a mad, thoughtless run – all high knees and floppy feet, limp arms flapping like a marionette.

I make it a respectable distance across the park, and I've still not been caught. Overly confident, I snatch a glance behind me. I've not been caught because the officer isn't chasing me. *Thank heavens, he isn't chasing me!* I think excitedly. Then I realise why the officer isn't chasing me. My mistake brings me screeching to a stop.

I've left the sack. I've left the bag. I've left Gwendolyn on the bench.

The officer is crouched over, peering inside.

'No! Wait, officer!' I call, sprinting back. The officer turns to look at me, furious, sickened at the sight he's seen. I skid to a stop a few feet from him, arms held out placatingly. 'Now, hear me out, good fellow.'

The officer does not hear me out. He rips his truncheon free and swings for me. I duck to one side and lurch for the bench. Seizing the sack, I spin back to the police officer just as a second truncheon swing is about to connect. Realising that he's about to bludgeon Gwendolyn, he pulls his weapon up and over at the last minute. He goes to sweep low for my legs, but I follow with the sack using it to cover my delicate shins. He moves his truncheon high and low searching for a strike, but I track him with my shield. I know. *I know.* I'm using Gwendolyn as a human shield. But what choice do I have? I came back for her, didn't I? *That has to count for something.*

I can see the officer getting impatient with this farcical truncheon game. He spreads his arms wide – I think he's going to tackle me! *Shit the bed. What do I do?!*

I take the top of the sack in two hands. Swinging it about my head, I lunge forward, trying to bludgeon the officer with Gwendolyn before he manages to pounce. Horrified at my weaponisation of the poor little girl, the officer ducks. Running on animal instinct I raise a knee, fast. It connects hard with the officer's ducking head. His legs give way, and he crumples to the ground, conked out.

FUUCCCKKKKKKKK.

I just assaulted a police officer. I knocked him out. There's a police officer that I just knocked out lying at my feet.

It's a shocking act I've committed. It cleanses me of that lesser animal instinct, and my natural, very human state of terror and panic settles back upon me. I grab the sack and run.

16

I shouldn't have come here. Not yet. I shouldn't be here. I may have jeopardised everything. But being out there was just as risky, wasn't it? That policeman wasn't supposed to be there... I should have turned back but it's too late now. As soon as I stepped inside, stepped on that fine carpet, it was too late. I'm not moving now. The carpets are moving for me. It's out of my hands now. I can't turn back. I took one step inside, one step on these carpets and they just carried me away. So plush. Such a rich, splendid green – transporting. You wouldn't understand, if you never walked on really lush carpet, you wouldn't understand. This building, these halls have the lushest of carpets. They've got me. I'm going. Star-tled, buttoned-up lackeys tried to stop me but they're no match, not for terrified Eggy and the fine green carpets.

I arrive at the door. The door to *the* room: Mr Mendelsohn's. It's a big grand door – as you would expect. I open it. I'm in.

Three sets of eyes seated at expansive intervals around a long table shoot my way. One set is old and dusty – Mr Mendelsohn; another set bitter and full of fury – Tabitha; the third set victorious – Terrence. He leans back in his chair at the far end of the table, his massive girth pooling around the arms of his seat. 'Perfect timing, Eggy. It's done. What's mine is mine.' A smile stretches across his gross face – cold and cruel. He spares me only a moment of his attention before returning to his meal. Globules of fat glisten from within the folds of his chins as he chomps down on half a roast chicken. Where'd the chicken come from?

'It's a *victory* chicken, Eggy. My personal feast. I am triumphant,' says Terrence, reading my mind.

I watch him suck noisily on a slippery leg, half-masticated meat tumbling and catching around his breasts and on top of the tiered rolls of fat that constitute his gut. I watch a piece fall and cling momentarily to the index knuckle of the hand that's wrapped around the chicken leg before sliding off and bouncing onto the expensive table, and it's as if someone turned on a tap and I'm washed in all those thoughts and feelings that flooded me in the sack back on the bench with Gwendolyn, before the officer spooked me into a less stable atmosphere.

Look at him. This cruel pig of a man. I came here, straight here, because I wanted him to help with… with… everything. *But he's the reason I need help with everything.* He's the one. He's ostracised me. He's tainted me. Stained me. He's jeopardised my freedom. *He's the one.*

Sunlight breaks through the cloud cover outside and spills through the tall sash windows lining one side of the room. I'm caught in its illumination. I find myself taking in the pleasant, sun-kissed image of London – a rare sight to behold – and it grips me savage. *London.* I like London. I want to be *in* with the city, not *out* of the city.

It's the *heat* of that thought that grips me.

That bloated shitting monster.

I want him to *suffer*, like me. I want him to relate. I want him to be filled with sorrow and regret for what he's done to me. I want him to *understand* what he's done. I want to wield power over him. I want to look down on him like a tyrannical god and say, 'Nobody fucks with Egbert Whistle' – but I can't, because they do. People do fuck with me, often. And as much as I'd like to be, I'm not a tyrannical god, I'm Eggy.

Motes of dust spotlighted by the sun's rays drift on unseen currents and collect around Terrence, pulled in by his gravity. I no longer want Terrence's help. I *want* to hurt him. I *want* to stop him. That's what I want. Now that I'm here, that's what I want.

Maybe if I took a moment I could study a page from his book, figure out how to wield some of that deadly leverage. But I'm having trouble focusing. I think I have the shaky quakes. I'm upset and I'm angry. I'm hurt and I'm angry. Terrence doesn't see it. He's not capable. And even if he were, he wouldn't because he's not looking at me. I've been dismissed from his thoughts. He lives for his half a roast victory chicken.

I take one step forward and I'm going for him. Throwing myself at him. I'm sliding headfirst down the long table toward Terrence situated at the far end. It's a grand table. *Mahogany*, I think as I shoot along, *well polished*. It's quite the distance to hurtle, but with a polish like this my destiny is assured.

I'm going to hurt him. I'm going to put an end to him. I want him to feel what I feel and then I want him to stop. Do you know what I mean? I have that *feeling*. It's a dangerous bloody feeling. You don't think much when you're shaking, your brain doesn't work right when it's quaking; the outer bits peel back and you find yourself moving from that stony core.

I'm hurtling straight for that nasty sack of greed. *Look at him.*

The first time I ever *wanted* to stop a person, properly stop them – are you with me? – was the first time I ever got the shaky quakes. Didn't go too well – ended up a hero. Won't happen this time though, now I've learnt the dangers. I'm all clued in. When you're shaking, shakingly quakingly angry, it's difficult to be accurate. That's why I'm going to get in close. Gnaw open that fatty fucking jugular and put his eyes out with my thumbs for good measure. I'm not thinking this though, you understand. I'm just feeling it. I'm feeling it all out, but that's where I'm at. Are you with me? That's where I am. Weapons, tools, are no good when you're quaking. Just close the distance and get stuck in.

That was my mistake at Passchendaele. Too much range. Too

much shaking. At first the shaking was good, a net positive. 'FIRE, WHISTLE. FIRE!' That's all it took, you know, and before I knew it – without thinking, just doing – I was looking right in the eyes of a very frightened young Englishman, a boy really, and before I knew it, I was pointing and shaking and pulling the trigger of my revolver. You should have seen the look, the look that boy had when he realised, you should have seen it.

I realised as soon as I saw the flash from the muzzle of my Webley, heard it go crack. That's when I realised. As soon as it was done, I knew it shouldn't be. It was too far, gone too far. It was a mistake.

I wanted to heave my insides out I was so sick. I couldn't face it. I could not face my mistake, but equally I couldn't resist the twisted curiosity to look. And when I looked, I discovered I was still looking at that boy's face, that very same face, still frightened but still alive. *I missed*. I missed the cheeky sod! I was weeping with joy. My hand had been shaking so much with everything that I missed. The look he had, the relief he had when I did… lasted all of two seconds. The moustache next to me, shouting 'FIRE, WHISTLE. FIRE!' – he didn't miss. He got him on the side, just above the boy's right ear. You should have seen that boy's face then.

That's when I got the shaky quakes. That's when I shook with anger, not with fear. It wasn't right, you know. I know because I tried it. I had tried to do what he did, and it wasn't right. It was wrong. It was wrong. The dead boy was right, and we were wrong. So, I took my Webley and pointed it at that bastard with the moustache. I pointed it right at him and fired. Unfortunately, with the shaky quakes, I missed. Shot a poor German chap sneaking up on him from behind. I tried again, tried to cave that top lip in with a solid piece of lead… but my shaking hand missed, again. Again, I shot another German chap sneaking up on the other side. Isn't that ironic? I got a medal for saving the life of the man I was trying to kill from the people who were trying to kill him. Classic Eggy, really.

I don't have a gun this time, so that's good, one less thing to worry about. I just need me.

Terrence can be quick, but not this time. I've slid too fast. Shot along like a table rocket. I strike. I wrap my fingers around the back of his fat head and dig my thumbs, hard as I can, into those piggy little eyes. At the same time, I sink my face into the creases of his hanging jowls, aiming for the neck. I bite through a layer of salty, crusted dirt smeared in fresh chicken juice before striking flesh. Taking a last breath through my nostrils, I press forward and burrow in. Pushing and gnawing inwards, searching for inner vitals; trying to tear and chew through his fleshy protections – fuck me, there's a *lot* of flesh.

Being so close, all I'm able to see is the granularity of Terrence's obese form, but on the outside of me, back out where daylight and clean air live, I become aware of Terrence pushing forward. Pushing me back onto the table and bearing down on me. I don't let up – I'm chewing for all my worth – but nor does Terrence. He's not pulling away. *Shit*. The big fat cunt isn't panicking. He's rallying. I feel the back of my head and shoulders collide with the tabletop. I have a momentary sensation of lying on my back, pinned to that finely polished mahogany, before being completely and utterly *consumed*. I feel every inch of me being squeezed and compressed as Terrence lies and heaves and surges down on top of me. *Shit*. He's not pulling away! He's pushing in. Pushing down with those great big jowls, choking me on that rank, foul-tasting flesh. I'm overwhelmed by the pressure – gravity naught but a footnote as the immense forces acting upon every plane of me squeeze out all sense of direction. There's no longer up nor down. There's only *in*. I'm being squeezed *in* on myself, as if to a singular point. Pressing home the advantage, Terrence stretches out his neck before forcing it further down and in, shoving more of his neck flesh into my mouth, sealing up my nose and sinking my eyeballs inwards. His riposte an attempt to choke me on his own fat before I manage to chew through his natural defences. I gnaw faster, harder, chomping towards a vein, an artery, anything mortal, knowing that it's victory or death.

My stomach and throat begin to spasm. My lungs shudder for air but, trapped under Terrence's titanic weight, there's simply no escape. Even if my resolve were to break, even if I should try to surface for a lungful of life-giving oxygen, the attempt would be entirely futile. The only path to survival is through, to bore teeth-first through Terrence's greed-filled neck meat. My whole body is trembling and juddering now, but my will remains unbroken.

Terrence is screaming, squealing, like a stuck pig – half pain, half malicious pleasure. My hands have given up on his pokey little eyes. They lie useless to the side, my fingertips just managing to escape the heavy reach of my victim's – my victor's – girth.

Tonguing a chunk of gnawed-off flesh into the pocket between teeth and cheek before it tumbles back and chokes me, I make to munch back down upon my enemy. But with all my fuel being just about spent, I find my body, my jaw, weakening. My masseter muscles failing me. Lactic acid rendering me useless.

My debilitations are pervasive, and I become an involuntary witness to my fading functions. I have no vision with which to register it, but I would imagine my external world's gone hazy and distant. My thoughts slow, quietening as the urgency of the situation begins to recede from my dimming consciousness. Somewhere on that shrinking periphery I just manage to catch the irony. It's something to do with gluttony and choking. And then I grow fainter.

If I could, I would – naturally – panic right now. But I can barely even think. At this point, I barely am. And if I *could* think, I'm sure my only thought would end up being '*I'm dying*', or something else equally as obvious as that.

Caused by a final deathly convulsion, I cramp up and clamp down reflexively on the blubber between my teeth. I remain like that, my jaw vice-like, as the last piece of me is overwhelmed… and off I drift. So long, Eggy!

17

Egbert Whistle is not dead. Egbert Whistle is alive. I spend a moment determining how I know that. And also wondering who this Egbert Whistle chap is. Then it comes to me that *I* am Egbert Whistle. I'm Eggy. But still remains the puzzle of how I know I'm not dead. The longer I puzzle on this the more pain I feel, and of course the clue is right there in my unadulterated agony. I know I'm alive because I'm full of hurt. That's a quintessential sign of life.

Aiming to prolong it, I gasp in oxygen. I quickly wish I hadn't bothered. My awareness expands along with my crushed lungs. In front of me is the ceiling, behind me a hard, smooth indifference, and a short distance above me, kneeling on the table, panting, bleeding profusely, is a man. The sight of that man returns to me the entirety of my situation. Oh Lordy. It would be better if I *were* dead, I fear.

The man, Terrence, yanks something from his neck and lets it drop. It tinkles across to me. Lordy. I think it's my tooth. Inspecting my mouth with my tongue I realise it could be one of many missing teeth. A sad comment on the condition of Terrence's leathery skin or my poor dental care, I know not.

'Did you enjoy that, you gloating bitch?' pants Terrence at, I assume, Tabitha. My awareness has now expanded to what I think is its full range, but Tabitha is located outside of it. I can't physically see her. I can't move. I'm alive but I'm too broken to move. All I can do is lie on my back, pancake-thin.

Terrence reaches behind him, towards me, grabs me by the hair and slides me up the table until I lie parallel with his knees. 'You think I'd lose to this washed-up fool?'

Now that Tear's moved me, I can see Tabitha at the very top of my vision. She stands at the far end of the table from where I began my slide. Behind her is the door. Still open. She's backlit by the gas lamps in the corridor beyond, her long shadow stretching all the way down to us. You wouldn't have thought that the early-morning light flooding in through the room's big windows would allow for such a bold shadow – I guess they've made an exception. It's a long shadow she casts but I was right, she is small. Small and slender, like a sparrow, but with a big old beak. A raven's weapon ready to rip my terror-drenched liver out, I'm sure. I'm really fucked here. There are two Chalamberts in the room, and I've betrayed both of them.

My eyes meet Tabitha's and my soul freezes in suspense.

Then she's turning, leaving.

'That's it, Tabitha, shuffle off back to your knitting. It was a nice play but you los*tht*. Goodbye,' taunts Terrence.

'Gwen-Gwen,' I moan, desperately trying to catch Tabitha's attention, to bring her back, but I'm struggling to form the right sounds. Something shifts inside my mouth, and I start to choke. I spit out the stored lump of neck. 'Gwendolyn,' I call again, successfully forming the whole name this time. It's still a mangled and pitifully weak sound I produce. Nevertheless, it just manages to latch. Terrence is quick to press his hand down on my mouth, to silence me, but that only helps to capture Tabitha's attention further. Terrence works harder to gag me, but he's as spent as I am and from between those fat fingers slips out, 'The sack! The sack!' As best I can, I gesture in the direction of the door. In my fury, I dropped it before my slide. 'The sack!' I gasp.

Tabitha spies something on the ground, starts to move toward it. Terrence's eyes go wide and the skin across his skull seems to shrink. He surges forward, crawling and scrabbling down the table as fast as his wearied, threadbare heart will let him. 'No. Wait! Wait, Tabitha!' he cries, but it's too late. It's done. Tabitha has the sack in her hands. It's open. She looks inside. Terrence freezes. The whole room freezes as a heart-stopping screech, a single hate-wrapped note pierces the air. Tabitha pulls away from the bag and the noise cuts off as abruptly as it started.

In the silence that follows, everyone and everything remains where they are for a stretched-out moment more, suspended at the climax. A moment of inertia before consequence bears down once more. Then there's a flash of hatred, a whirl of skirt and scarf, and Tabitha's on the table, rushing down its surface, in her hand a *knife*. She flies along, as if on strings, the feet beneath her skirts hardly seeming to move, her arm outstretched with that wicked point. And before Terrence, that worn-out, spent-up monster of a man, can move, he finds himself pierced – a dagger stuck with expert precision in his left breast.

There it remains as Tabitha withdraws. Terrence takes it in: he takes in Tabitha panting before him, her face filled with unre-morseful loathing. Carefully, he climbs unsteadily to his feet, tottering a few steps down the table before gaining control. I'm still on my back as Terrence looms over the room. Then, as if it were little more than a thorn pricking his clothing, he pulls the dagger from his breast and casually drops it. It clatters on the wood. I get a good look at it. *That's a shame.* It's only small, a glorified pen-knife at best. Given the layers of blubberous protection that surround him, I doubt it even reached the ribs, let alone his organs.

'That…' begins Terrence with a sneer, and then stops. He seizes up, rigid from head to toe, the hand that retrieved the knife clutching at his heart. And just like before, he topples forward stiff as a board, headfirst onto the tabletop… only Tabitha finds herself caught in the middle. There's a sickening crunch of bones and she's gone, buried beneath Terrence.

I wait. I wait longer but Terrence doesn't move, doesn't breathe, doesn't twitch. Still on my back, too weary, too wary to raise myself up, to expose myself like that, I use my feet to push and slide myself quietly, horizontally and with great trepidation along the table. I stop when Terrence's eyes come into view. His eyes are open, but they're glassy and lifeless. For the second time this morning, I go searching for a pulse. I reach forward cautiously and press two fingers to his neck. They're instantly soiled in blood and I remember that, of course, his neck's a ghastly mess. I reach down to his wrist instead, seeking a pulse – or rather, confirming the absence of one. I find nothing there.

Fuck me. I think he's dead. Dead. The horrible cunt is actually dead.

I painfully remove myself from the horizontal, rolling and pitching to my knees. Although reluctant to touch Terrence any further lest he surge frighteningly back to life, I heave against his side. The physical effort is agony. I manage to roll him up and over just an inch but it's enough. With my shoulder set against his bulk, I use both hands to yank on Tabitha. I manage to clear her out to the waist before I give in. I rather wish I hadn't. She's dead too. Her ribs have splintered through the bodice of her dress and her left elbow has been turned inside out, pointing in the wrong direction. Most tellingly of all, her neck's snapped.

'Good lord, Mr Whistle. I think they're dead,' comes a voice that sounds like dry old leaves. My heart almost jumps out of my chest. My head spins round looking for the source. It's Jenkins. Jenkins! The long-suffering servant to the Chalambert family. Where the hell did he come from? *Has he been here this whole time?* I *really* have to learn to be more observant.

18

I'm stood on the platform at Victoria waiting for my train. Jenkins is with me. Followed me here like a lost dog. You'll never believe it, but he was in the room the whole time. Sat in the corner twiddling his senile thumbs. Yet even more surprising were the actions of Mr Mendelsohn – or rather, lack thereof. The entire time I was gnawing on Tear, and then right through the stabbing, the falling and the crushing of Tabitha, he never moved. Never lifted a finger. Never batted an eyelid. Which makes you wonder, what else has he seen at a Chalambert gathering that this shouldn't even raise an eyebrow?

I'm pulled away from pondering the curious Mr Mendelsohn and his strange world by that mind-numbing thought that refuses to process: Terrence is dead. *My Tear Bear is dead.*

I know I just tried to kill him. I am aware that, not more than an hour ago, I tried to open up his jugular with my teeth, but regardless, it's horribly shocking. Tabitha is dead too. I didn't really know her, but, as I'd hope you can imagine, that's also quite shocking.

Disquieted, I stare through the gloom looking for my train. I'm in a right old pickle now: the only people who would (or could, at least) have been able to clean up the mess I'm in – the Bridewaters, the nuns, the grandma, the papers, the incident at the hospital, the dead girl in a sack, the police officer, and the attempted murder of Terrence – are both dead.

The puissant combination of the dead Chalamberts and the shock of seeing Jenkins appear from nowhere had compelled me to hurl myself through the window of Mr Mendelsohn's office, but at the last moment that devilish sin curiosity got the better of me.

Mr Mendelsohn informed me – or rather he looked through me and spoke as if he were announcing the shipping forecast – that should Terrence Chalambert pass away before naming an heir, the estate was to pass to Ms Chalambert. Tabitha. I explained to the peculiar man that Tabitha, laying under Tear with the clearly shattered ribs and broken neck, was also dead.

He spent some time rifling through his papers before stating, as chance would have it, that should both Chalamberts pass before naming an heir the estate was to be held in trust until the darling of the Chalambert family should come of age: one Miss Gwendolyn Richmond.

'Dead, too,' I regrettably informed him.

There was yet more paper shuffling and dry breathing before Mr Mendelsohn announced that the Chalambert estate was to pass to Senior Chalambert's most faithful and trusted companion – at which point I thought 'Oh, *fuck me, don't name a family pet. He's about to name a bloody dog*' – but it was worse than that, he named Mr William Jenkins.

Jenkins, the geriatric man stood next to me who has more liver spots than he does brain cells, has in the stroke of a pen become one of the wealthiest men in Britain.

I turn and look at him, wondering if he knew? Wondering if he, Jenkins, somehow masterminded all of this? Wondering if he's not in fact a doddering invalid but actually a cunning, deceptive, Machiavellian genius. But then I watch him trying to light an empty tobacco pipe with an unlit match and figure that no, he's definitely just a jammy bastard.

I reach into his pocket and take out his tobacco tin. Thumbing it in place, I light the match.

'Thank you, Mr Whistle. Guess I should get used to this, hey?'

I don't know if he's speaking with humour or delusions. Either way, I decide to strike him. But lifting my arm causes pain to lance through my shoulder and I give in.

'I say, sir, I know you're in spot of bother right now, but once it all blows over I'd be honoured if you'd come work for me?'

'Work for you? Bloody hell. Doing what?'

'Well, you see, sir, it's always been a dream of mine to breed horses, thoroughbreds, for the races and whatnot. I'll need someone to handle the business side of it, I imagine.' The nightmarish image of a dead Julius trots through my exhausted mind.

The train pulls into the platform amid great billows of smoke. 'You're a dangerous fool, Jenkins. If you know what's good for you, you'll stay well away from horses.' I pat my pocket containing the train ticket and the wad of cash I made Jenkins part with. He was highly reluctant. It's his pension for the month. He's sceptical he'll actually see any of the Chalamberts' money. And well he should be; the rats will be crawling out of the woodwork now.

'Is this you, sir?'

I nod.

'Where to?'

I pull open the carriage door – first class, naturally – and gingerly ascend the steps. 'Switzerland. I saved a man's life once, last I heard that's where he retired to.'

'You think he'll help you, sir?'

I look down at Jenkins from the top step of the carriage. 'He shan't have any choice, Jenkins. It's all about leverage, you see. It'd do you well to learn that.'

The End

ABOUT THE AUTHOR

Alister lives in New York's Hudson Valley with his wife and dog.

Gentlemen Don't Run is his debut novel. He's writing another. If you'd like to be kept up to date about any future book releases you can sign up to email updates here:

www.alisteraustin.com/writer

Printed in Great Britain
by Amazon